He led her up to the main deck that was open. They walked hand in hand as the sun finished slipping down below the horizon and the first stars began to creep out.

Lacey stared up at the sky. "So beautiful."

And he had to agree, but it wasn't the stars that he was looking at. "Have you ever seen the northern lights?"

"Yes, but not for some time. I hope we'll see some the farther north we go."

"I hope so, too."

She was so beautiful, and as they stood there stargazing, he reached out and touched her cheek. A pink blush crept up her neck, and he felt goose bumps break out over her soft skin. She bit her bottom lip, her big eyes looking up at him through thick lashes.

He couldn't resist. He pulled her into his arms and tasted her lips.

Softly at first. His hands were in her hair as she pressed closer, the kiss deepening as he drank her taste in.

Dear Reader,

Thank you for picking up a copy of Lacey and Thatcher's story, *Falling for His Runaway Nurse*.

I've always wanted to go on an Alaskan cruise. Anyone who knows me knows I love the north, and so this was a fun setting for my characters.

Lacey is a runaway bride. Her fiancé cheated on her, and she has to escape and clear her mind, and there's nothing more relaxing than a cruise. Even better, she gets to work as a nurse, which will keep her busy and her mind off her ex's betrayal.

Thatcher has been hiding from his birthright as the next Duke of Weyburn and from the pain of his past. All he wants to do is disappear into the Klondike and practice medicine in a remote community.

On his last cruise he runs into his new nurse, Lacey, who stands there in her wedding dress. Neither are looking for love, but love always finds a way!

I hope you enjoy Lacey and Thatcher's story.

I love hearing from readers, so please visit my website, www.amyruttan.com, or give me a shout on Twitter, @ruttanamy.

With warmest wishes,

Amy Ruttan

FALLING FOR HIS
RUNAWAY NURSE

AMY RUTTAN

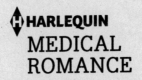

HARLEQUIN

MEDICAL
ROMANCE

HARLEQUIN®
MEDICAL
ROMANCE™

Recycling programs
for this product may
not exist in your area.

ISBN-13: 978-1-335-40882-2

Falling for His Runaway Nurse

Copyright © 2021 by Amy Ruttan

This edition published by arrangement with Harlequin Books S.A.

For questions and comments about the quality of this book,
please contact us at CustomerService@Harlequin.com.

Harlequin Enterprises ULC
22 Adelaide St. West, 40th Floor
Toronto, Ontario M5H 4E3, Canada
www.Harlequin.com

Printed in U.S.A.

Born and raised just outside Toronto, Ontario, **Amy Ruttan** fled the big city to settle down with the country boy of her dreams. After the birth of her second child, Amy was lucky enough to realize her lifelong dream of becoming a romance author. When she's not furiously typing away at her computer, she's mom to three wonderful children, who use her as a personal taxi and chef.

Books by Amy Ruttan

Harlequin Medical Romance

First Response
Pregnant with the Paramedic's Baby

Cinderellas to Royal Brides
Royal Doc's Secret Heir

NY Doc Under the Northern Lights
Carrying the Surgeon's Baby
The Surgeon's Convenient Husband
Baby Bombshell for the Doctor Prince
Reunited with Her Hot-Shot Surgeon
A Reunion, a Wedding, a Family
Twin Surprise for the Baby Doctor
Falling for the Billionaire Doc

Visit the Author Profile page
at Harlequin.com for more titles.

In memory of my mother-in-law
and her dream trip to Alaska.

We miss you, Barb.

CHAPTER ONE

"WELL, WE DO need a nurse…"

Lacey smiled and nodded. She knew that the recruitment officer was staring at her—not that she really could blame her—but tried to stay positive. It was a bit of an odd situation, even for her. Well, it was completely odd to her. Lacey didn't particularly like taking risks. She didn't like change or waste.

Things usually ran smoothly in her life, especially when it came to her career.

She planned everything she could.

Like her wedding and that expensive cake that she had shelled out for.

What a waste.

She didn't even get to taste it.

That's because you ran out on your wedding.

Lacey shook that thought away and smiled brightly, smoothing out the tulle on her dress. Not that smoothing it over would diminish its volume, but the sensation of running her hands over the fabric calmed her and stopped her leg from nervously tapping under the table.

"I know my dress is a bit of a surprise."

The human resources woman pushed her glasses back up the bridge of her nose and smiled politely. "You can call me Deb and, I'll be honest, it *is* unusual. After all, it's not often that we have candidates come to an interview in a wedding dress."

Lacey blushed. "It's a long story. I was in something of a hurry to get here."

That was an understatement. When she had walked in on her fiancé in a compromising position with her maid of honor, she had needed to make a run for it.

So she did. She bolted, completely unprepared for what came next, which was so unlike her.

"I can see that." Deb cleared her throat. "Well, your credentials are outstanding, and everything you've provided checked out. We're also in a bind as we urgently need a nurse practitioner for this three-week cruise—though the placement is four weeks in total for staff as they come back with the ship. Not sure we'll need your midwife certification, but you never know."

Lacey smiled nervously. "Well, I do love babies."

She did, but when she'd moved to Vancouver five years ago, there had only been a job in the emergency room, so she became a trauma nurse and put her midwife career on the back burner. She missed it so much.

It was in the ER that she had met Will. He told her she was a great trauma nurse. He told her that the emergency room needed her.

That he needed her.

Lacey swallowed the lump in her throat.

"Welcome aboard, Ms. Greenwood. I'm so very glad that you're able to sail with us this afternoon, though I do hope we don't have any babies born on ship," Deb said, interrupting Lacey's thoughts.

Lacey breathed out a sigh of relief. "Thank you!"

"If you'll follow me, we'll board, and I'll show you the medical facilities. We do provide a uniform and scrubs, but I presume you have other clothes in that suitcase. I know it's summer, but Alaska still has its nippy days."

Lacey glanced back at her suitcase—the one she had packed for her honeymoon—but instead of feeling sad about the honeymoon she wasn't going to get, she just felt anger and a bit of distance. But most of all, disappointment that she had been duped.

Again.

When it came to love, she was cursed. She always picked the wrong guy. Ones who left her, cheated on her—and one time, one who stole most of her clothing. It was hard to trust men when they had a habit of always breaking her heart.

Just like her fiancé. Or rather, her ex-fiancé.

She was angry at herself for not seeing the signs earlier. She didn't want to believe that once again, she'd got it wrong. That she had—foolishly—almost walked down the aisle and gotten married to a man who lied and had cheated on her.

Will had seemed like a stable guy. Someone she could settle down with, who was just as much of a workaholic as she was.

She had thought he was a safe bet. Someone who could make her *feel* safe for one moment in her life.

Did you?

Lacey shook that thought away. She knew she had been stagnating in her work, happy to go along with Will's plans to stay in Vancouver and maintain the status quo. But there had always been a small part of her that had wanted change. She had thought marriage would be that change.

Apparently, that wasn't meant to be.

Before Vancouver Lacey had spent so many years of her life bouncing from one place to the other, making her crave stability.

Or so she'd thought.

She liked Will well enough and thought what they had was enough for a successful marriage.

Their relationship was comfortable. It wasn't needy. They both agreed that work came first.

It was okay.

And so she had asked him to marry her. It seemed like the right thing to do. The natural progression. None of her previous relationships had lasted that long before. She'd never stayed put for so long.

And wasn't marriage the step that everyone took eventually?

Being settled with Will was the only time in her life she'd had a sense of stability and peace since her family had lived in Yellowknife when she was younger. When she'd had a real best friend.

Carol.

Another lump formed in her throat as she blinked back tears. Carol had been like family, but she'd died last year just before Lacey got engaged. Lacey had been devastated, and had been grateful that she had the wedding to focus on to help her get through her grief.

She'd had Will.

Now she didn't.

She should've trusted her gut.

On a whim, she'd decided to see him before the ceremony, because she didn't really believe in that silly custom of the groom not seeing the bride before the wedding. That's when she caught him in the act, with her friend Beth.

It brought to the surface all those signs she'd been ignoring because she thought Will was perfect for her. Stable.

She'd wanted that stability so badly.

Did you?

She'd been blind, and seeing Will with Beth was a wake-up call.

Instead of waiting to hear all the same excuses she'd heard from others in the past, she marched out of the room, grabbed her suitcase and caught the first taxi she could to take her as far away from Will as possible.

The taxi driver drove her around for an hour as she figured out what she wanted to do—all she knew was she needed an escape—and as the cab passed the docks, she saw all the waiting cruise ships. Lacey remembered there had been an opening for a nurse practitioner on one of them. She had only been casually looking at the postings—though she realized now it hadn't actually been all that casual—and it had caught her eye.

When she showed it to Will, he'd scoffed. He didn't see the point.

"Why would you want to do that?" he'd asked.

"Why not? It's an adventure. We can use a

break, and heading north to Alaska sounds exciting."

Will had made a face. "North? Exciting? Those two words don't go together."

"Sure they do. I lived in Yellowknife. It's wonderful."

Will had shaken his head and ended the discussion with a firm, "No. Not at this time. We're busy. Things are good here."

Lacey had agreed—Will was right. Vancouver was safer—but there was a part of her, one she'd tried hard to suppress, that still wanted to go. She wanted to travel up north again.

It called to her.

The one time when she'd been truly settled as a child had been when her father had been stationed in Yellowknife.

She'd never stayed long enough in one place to have a best friend before, but this time they did, and she'd met Carol. That had been the happiest time in her life.

Alaska was far from Yellowknife, but it was an escape.

Right then, an escape was exactly what she needed. Time for herself and to figure out what she really wanted. She was going nowhere in her career. She missed midwifery. The emergency room kept her busy, but all she did was work, and obviously her personal life was doing the same. She was stuck in a rut.

Lacey wasn't sure what she wanted anymore, but she knew what she needed—adventure. And fast.

Applying for a job on a month-long Alaskan cruise seemed like the right thing to do.

In theory.

She pulled herself back to the present, realizing Deb was still waiting on an answer.

"I have clothes, Deb. Don't worry." There was no point in getting into the details about her canceled honeymoon, and she had everything she needed to get by. She'd already texted her dad and asked him to get her stuff from Will's place, so there was nothing holding her back from disappearing for a few weeks.

She was free, and it was a bit unnerving. In fact, she was shaking, her heart was racing, and she was already beginning to second-guess this decision.

"Oh, good, because I do have to warn you that Dr. Bell probably won't take too kindly to the outfit."

Lacey noticed Deb kind of winced, but still had a smile on her face, which Lacey could only deduce meant one thing. Dr. Bell was most likely a bit of a stubborn mule.

Lacey could deal with a doctor like that.

She had a lot of experience dealing with grumpy surgeons.

Her father was a Royal Canadian Mounted Police officer, and he'd taught her how to be strong. As they'd moved from place to place all over Canada for his work, she had learned how to grow a thick skin. She'd also learned to live in some of the most remote places in the north, and if it didn't faze her as a kid she wasn't going to start letting it bother her now.

She could handle this.

There was nothing to be nervous about. This temporary job was just a chance to clear her head and decide what to do when she returned to Vancouver, because she already knew that she wasn't leaving Vancouver just because Will had betrayed her.

Her parents were there.

They were her only roots now.

Lacey pulled her suitcase behind her as she followed Deb out of the office and up a gangway that led onto the ship. It was a staff entrance and didn't have the same fanfare as the main gangway that would soon be full of tourists embarking on a dream cruise. There were no crew greeting her, no free drinks and warm reception. Just a narrow hall and busy crew members getting everything ready for departure.

She knew this cruise was work—her means

to escape the reality she was now facing and the fact her life had gone so wrong—but she had to admit that a free drink would really hit the spot right now.

"I'll take you to the clinic so you can meet the doctor. I still have to figure out your room assignment, though, and get you identification so you can open doors only accessed by staff," Deb said over her shoulder as they made their way through the maze of hallways.

As far as Lacey was concerned, the sooner they left, the better, even though right now her nerves were shot and her stomach seemed to be doing backflips in her abdomen.

Lacey just wanted to get to work and forget this whole day had ever happened.

She wanted to forget the shock of finding Will and Beth together. She wanted to forget how foolish she felt to have missed the signs that she and Will were not actually compatible.

She was hurt, angry and numb.

Finally they arrived at the infirmary.

"This is where you'll be working with Dr. Bell." Deb knocked, but didn't wait for anyone to answer as she walked in. "Dr. Bell, I have a replacement nurse for you."

Dr. Bell came out of an exam room, ducking because he was at least six foot and the doorway was not. His dark gray eyes were stormy, he was scowling and his ginger hair was a bit mussed, like he'd been raking his fingers through it in frustration. The white uniform suited him, and before she could help herself, she found she was checking him out from head to toe.

What are you doing?

Her cheeks grew hot in embarrassment. She had no idea what had come over her. All she could think of was how frazzled she felt—her heart was racing and her blood was heated. She just hoped she wasn't blushing.

This was so silly.

She'd just walked out on a wedding. Now was not the time to be admiring her new boss.

Still, Lacey was zapped with a rush of something she hadn't felt in a long time. In fact, she couldn't recall ever feeling or experiencing this kind of visceral reaction before. It seemed right and was mixed with a sense of familiarity too. As though she'd seen him before.

She couldn't quite put her finger on it, but she felt as if she knew him.

Get a grip.

It didn't matter where she'd seen him before.

She was here to work and figure out why she kept falling for men who cheated on her. Whatever momentary attraction she'd felt for Dr. Bell was wrong.

Even if he was very dashing, he was her boss, and she was fresh off an almost-marriage.

That was a recipe for disaster.

In a British accent, he began, "It's about bloody time..." He paused when he saw her, and his lips pursed together. "I asked for a nurse, Deb, not a wife!"

This was not what he was expecting.

Thatcher had been worried he wouldn't have a nurse on this trip. He'd felt so flustered about potentially not having support staff that he'd answered a call from his brother.

Something he never did.

Thatcher had been annoyed with himself, especially when it was clear Michael was angry, spending several minutes grousing over the fact he'd had to hire a private investigator to locate him. A fact that made Thatcher livid.

So instead of a normal conversation, Thatcher had to endure a thirty-minute guilt session on how he'd abandoned the family and the title and that their father was ill. So now more than ever he needed to get married and produce heirs. Thatcher tried that once. It didn't work.

He didn't want the title. And harsh as it sounded, he didn't want to see his father. All Thatcher wanted was his medical career, to stay and settle in Canada and to do so without his father's help.

It had always been his goal to make his own way, buy some land in the Yukon and set up a practice in a small community where no one knew his father was the Duke of Weymouth and that he was next in line to inherit the estate and title.

A place where no one would eventually call him "Your Grace."

That was his dream.

The cruise ship gig was just a job to get him the funds so that he could purchase the land— the means to the end—and after this cruise, he would have all he needed to live out his dream. As long as nothing screwed it up, that is. He just needed this to be a smooth and uneventful trip.

And then Michael had called and nagged him about not settling down and taking up his birth-right. As if being married and procreating was all that he was good for to his family. Were they stuck in some kind of Regency-era book?

It wasn't for lack of trying that Thatcher wasn't married. A wife and kids were things he'd always wanted. The kind of loving family he'd never had growing up.

He'd been close once, but it turned out Kathleen didn't want *him*. All she wanted was to be a duchess.

Thatcher didn't want to be the duke if it meant turning out like his father.

Distant.

Cold.

Uncaring.

When his mother was sick and dying, the most compassionate, kindest person had been her physician. His father wasn't there, but the doctor was.

And that was why Thatcher had wanted to become a doctor. He wanted to save lives.

Only, Kathleen didn't share in that dream.

She wanted the aristocracy and the money that went along with it.

She didn't love him, and when it became clear he was serious about moving to Canada, she left him. After that, he'd moved, changed his name to his mother's surname and avoided women altogether.

Thatcher fell in love with the Yukon and Canada and convinced himself it was easier to live out his dream single.

Except you're lonely.

He shook that thought away. Even though he'd always longed for a family, a wife, he couldn't trust a woman to want him for him.

So he gave up on all that.

Now here he was, staring down a bride. And a beautiful one at that.

Was this some kind of cruel twist of fate or karma or whatever?

"I'm Lacey Greenwood. Your new nurse." She smiled brightly and stuck out her hand.

Thatcher looked her up and down.

She was enchanting.

He couldn't deny that. Her honey-blond hair was done up in a bun with a few loose strands. Her blue eyes twinkled and her lips were full, pink. They were made for kissing.

Don't.

He was shocked that she was standing there in a wedding dress. Was she fresh from her wedding ceremony? Was she a jilted bride?

She didn't look all that heartbroken.

There were no red splotches on her creamy skin, no puffy eyes to hint that she'd been crying. And while she wore an engagement ring, there was no wedding ring on her finger.

Maybe she was the jilter?

"Are you indeed?" he finally said, breaking the silence, but not taking her hand. "What qualifications and experience do you have?"

The smile on her face slipped, and her big blue eyes narrowed. He knew he was making Deb uncomfortable too. He hated being an old crank, but he wasn't going to let anything ruin his last cruise.

He just wanted things to go smoothly and calmly.

He didn't need some flighty runaway bride as his nurse.

Especially such an attractive one. He found himself wondering what was under all that tulle...

No, you don't!

"I'm a registered nurse practitioner and certified midwife. Deb has all of my credentials," she stated firmly.

Thatcher raised his eyebrows. She had spirit. He liked that.

No, you don't.

"Dr. Bell, I did my due diligence," Deb started, flustered. "Nurse Greenwood is more than capable."

He felt a pang of guilt for being disrespectful to Deb. He'd honestly forgotten she was there. All he saw was Lacey.

Lacey frowned. "I'm more than qualified, Dr. Bell. Are you going to be so pigheaded to let something as silly as a wedding dress hold up the cruise? I'm not going into lengthy explanations about why I'm wearing a wedding dress, because that's my business, but I can assure you it won't affect my work."

"Are you lecturing me?" he asked, amused.

No one stood up to him, not usually, and he kind of liked it.

No. You. Don't, that inner voice reminded him again. It was setting off danger flares.

Lacey crossed her arms. "I am."

"Fine." He sighed in resignation. He didn't want the cruise postponed, and he was sure Deb had vetted her properly. "You can stay, I suppose."

Deb looked visibly relieved. "Well, now that it's all settled, I'll just take Lacey to meet the captain, get her identification and show her to her quarters."

"I expect you back here at seventeen hundred hours to report for duty, Nurse Greenwood. That's five o'clock, if you're not used to military time."

She screwed up her eyes, and she smiled, saluting him. "Aye, aye."

Thatcher chuckled to himself as Deb led Lacey out of the infirmary and down the hall. He peeked out the door to watch her walk away, pulling her suitcase behind her.

Her tulle skirt took up the entire width, and he smiled again. It was comical.

This is your last cruise. Remember? Focus on that.

He shook his head and shut the door. Thatcher

was hoping for smooth sailing, but with Nurse Lacey Greenwood working with him, this would likely be a choppy voyage indeed.

CHAPTER TWO

GRUMPY JERK-FACE.

Lacey opened her suitcase and began packing away her clothes and toiletries in the wardrobe that was in her cabin. She had a very small room, but Deb had told her at least it had its own bathroom and a porthole, unlike the interior cabins, so that was something. And right now, the way she was feeling, she was glad that she wasn't sharing a cabin with anyone.

She needed her own space to think, as she was having a hard time gathering her thoughts. Especially after meeting Dr. Bell.

Lacey slammed her suitcase shut and glanced out her porthole at Vancouver.

It might not be the best view on the ship, but she wasn't here as a tourist, and clearly it wasn't going to be any kind of vacation working with Dr. Thatcher Bell. She was here to work. When he crossed through her mind again, her heart fluttered and warmth crept up her neck.

He made her nervous, and she'd never been this skittery around a boss before.

What was wrong with her? Why was she reacting this way?

She'd been surprised when she heard the British accent. She was a bit of a sucker for a British accent. It always made her heart skip a beat.

You need to stop.

She zipped up her suitcase in frustration.

She had to keep reminding herself to work and figure out her life.

Not indulge an inappropriate attraction to her new boss.

Lacey couldn't remember the last time she had been so struck with instant attraction when she met a man.

With Will, she'd thought he was cute, and after she'd had some disastrous relationships, she liked that he was open and honest—or so she'd thought.

All she'd ever wanted was stability.

Something constant.

She wanted roots and to raise a family. Will had made it clear kids weren't in the plans anytime soon, and so she'd put that thought out of her mind too, even though it was important to her.

She should have taken that for the warning

sign it was that her relationship with Will was doomed from the get-go.

Was she so obsessed with safety that she was willing to settle?

Still, she never expected him to cheat on her. Especially not with someone she considered her best friend in Vancouver.

That hurt, but not as much as it should.

And that thought was sobering.

What is wrong with me?

When had she become so numb?

She wasn't a romantic and didn't believe in the whole "one true love and soul mate" nonsense. If she believed in that, she'd go insane. People you loved left you. Or you had to leave them. She knew that better than most.

Her heart ached as she thought of Carol. Will hadn't gone to the funeral, leaving Lacey to face it alone. Another red flag she'd ignored.

The pain of losing Carol had scared her.

It's why she proposed to Will. She wanted a family of her own—a net of security if something happened to her parents, the only family and roots she had left.

When exactly had she stopped believing in the fairy tale and become so pragmatic?

She wasn't sure, but she was sure of one thing…she'd dodged a bullet by not marrying Will. And she was glad she ran when she did.

Although it terrified her. She didn't like the uncertainty of not knowing what her next steps would be. It made her stomach turn. Just like when she was a kid and her dad would talk about a new posting, the uneasiness about the unknown that always settled in the pit of her stomach was back.

Working this Alaska trip and buying herself time to make a plan was exactly what she needed. Even if it meant working for the dishy ginger British doctor.

Just thinking about him and the way he'd looked her up and down caused a shudder of anticipation to run down her spine. It was lust, it was need and it was a level of want that she'd never experienced before.

It was kind of unnerving, and she hated herself for feeling this way. That wasn't why she was here. Only, she couldn't help but think of him and that visceral fire he ignited in her. It was almost like she'd never really seen a man before. It was like she'd been asleep, and now she was awake.

Don't think like that. You're here to work.

She had to keep reminding herself of that.

Alaska was always on her bucket list, and it was a perfectly timed escape when she needed it, but this was a job, and she was a professional. She prided herself on her work, and she was going to make sure that Dr. Thatcher Bell knew she was one of the best nurses there was. She was going to impress him. And then, while she was working, she could figure out what she wanted to do next when she got back to Vancouver.

Not having a plan made her nervous, but she was sure she could figure something out soon.

Lacey finished folding the rest of her clothes and then changed out of the wedding dress, which she shoved into the back of the small closet, behind her suitcase.

She cleaned up a bit, wiping off the wedding makeup and brushing out her hair, opting for a simple bun rather than the intricate updo that had been done for her veil and tiara.

The white dress uniform was a bit weird and different from her usual scrubs, but the entire staff wore it, and she would have to get used to it. She glanced down at her hand, saw the engagement ring there.

Even though she had popped the question to Will, he'd still bought her a simple ring. It had been a romantic gesture, but she was annoyed by it right now because it had obviously meant nothing to him, and now it was even more of a reminder of what a farce the whole wedding idea had been.

Yet she couldn't bring herself to take it off.

There was a knock at the door.

"Come in," Lacey said, straightening her uniform.

Deb opened the door and smiled. "You look much better."

Lacey laughed. "I suppose it would look strange to be walking around the ship in that gown."

"Just a bit. I have your identification tags and some scrubs. You only have to wear the white uniform when we're in port or in the evening if the captain has his staff at his table."

"Do we eat with the captain every night?" Lacey asked.

"No, not every night. Just when the captain asks his senior staff to join him."

"Am I senior staff?" Lacey asked, puzzled.

"Yes. You and Dr. Bell are the only medical staff on this ship."

"Okay." She had never been referred to as senior staff before. She'd had a promotion and she hadn't even done anything yet.

Deb nodded. "Well, I better go make sure that everything is prepped for sailing. As we leave port, it's expected that everyone goes on deck, but Dr. Bell can guide you. Departure is at five thirty."

"That sounds great. Thank you, Deb."

"No. Thank you for coming and taking on

the job so quickly. You've gotten us out of a real bind." Deb left, and Lacey clipped her identification tags on.

There was also a deck map in the pile of documents Debra had handed her, which she really appreciated.

It was going to take her some time to figure out this ship. She glanced at the alarm clock in her room, and as it was getting close to the time she had to report for duty, she grabbed what she needed, checked that her hair was neat and left her quarters.

She studied the map to remind herself where the infirmary was and made her way through the narrow passages to the staff stairwell. The higher she climbed, the more she could hear the happy passengers boarding the ship. She could feel the excitement of travel in the air.

It made her a bit anxious, but in a good way this time.

She couldn't wait until they pulled out of port and she was waving goodbye to Vancouver for the next month.

Then she would be able to breathe easier.

She made her way to the infirmary and took a deep breath before she opened the door. Sure, Dr. Bell might be hard to work with, but she'd dealt with worse. It was the attraction she was feeling toward him that she had to get control of.

That pull.

One she'd never dealt with before, and it was unwelcome and distracting. She wanted none of that.

Don't you?

"Nurse Greenwood reporting for duty, sir." She saluted as he casually turned around to look at her with indifference.

"You don't need to salute. I'm not the captain," he replied stiffly.

"Ah, but you are my commanding officer."

He frowned. "It's fine when the bridge crew is around, but down here I like to keep things informal, like a real clinic."

"Aren't we a real clinic, though?" she asked.

"Are you going to be flippant with me the whole voyage?" he asked despondently.

"Sorry, sir."

"Dr. Bell is fine. Even Thatcher is preferable."

"Okay, if we're going by first names, you can call me Lacey."

A strange expression crossed his face. "It's a strange name, isn't it?"

"What?"

"Lacey. I've never heard of it before."

"No weirder than Thatcher, which I thought was just a surname," she replied.

A smile tugged on the corner of his lips, briefly. "Deb gave me a copy of your curriculum vitae. You have outstanding references and credentials. You walked away from quite the impressive job at Vancouver General. Why?"

She crossed her arms. "I'd rather not get into that."

"Were you fired?"

She tried not to roll her eyes. "You can see I wasn't. I quit."

"Yes. Quite quickly. So, do tell me why you left."

"It's personal," she responded stiffly.

"Oh?" He cocked his eyebrow and leaned against the exam table. "So it has something to do with the wedding."

"Obviously."

His gray eyes landed on her hand. "Well, you're still wearing the engagement ring, so I'm assuming he ended it."

"I don't appreciate you being so flippant. Haven't you ever had your heart broken before?"

A strange look crossed his face. "Yes. You're right. I'm sorry. Please accept my apologies."

"Apology accepted." She stared at him, and once again she could've sworn she'd seen him before. She couldn't take her eyes off him as she tried to figure it out.

"What?" he asked, his back straightening.

"It's nothing. You just look vaguely familiar. That's all."

The moment the words slipped past her lips, his expression hardened and he turned away.

"I don't know what you're talking about," he groused.

It's probably better to drop it.

The last thing she wanted to do was make things even worse.

"So, what is the first thing we have to do? This is my first voyage, and Deb mentioned something about having to go on deck as the ship leaves port."

He nodded, but still didn't turn around to look at her. "Yes. The captain runs through a safety protocol."

"Okay, well, you'll have to guide me."

He finally turned around. "We'll go up on deck together. We'll have to guide people out. Just stick by me."

"Great. Look, I know the circumstances of how I came to work here are a bit odd, but I'm willing to work hard if you just give me a chance."

That was the understatement of the year.

Still, Thatcher couldn't fault her for the circumstances that brought her on board, and was thankful Deb had found her.

Even if she was tempting. And God knew he didn't need to be tempted. He might be lonely, but he had no intention of ever getting married.

He also wasn't a fling sort of person. A one-night stand wasn't for him.

What bothered him was the way she looked at him. It was worrying that she seemed to recognize him. He just hoped that she didn't actually know who he was. Not everyone read the tabloids or kept up with the British aristocracy. Still, when he'd left England, the rumors of his disappearance from the social scene had been rampant, and his picture had been plastered everywhere. Why would an heir to a dukedom just up and leave?

It was five years ago, but he knew he was still appearing in the occasional royal magazine. He was used to showing up in those rags quite a bit when he still had to attend events like the horse races at Royal Ascot and diplomatic receptions for foreign royals and dignitaries.

When he still wore suits and had the glamorous Kathleen on his arm.

When the whole world watched him simply because of his birthright.

He'd had a few close calls since he moved to Canada and took up this job on the cruise ship—passengers coming close to realizing who he was. Thankfully, though, no one who worked on the ship had recognized him, and he knew that no one would bother him when he was finally able to move onto his own land up north.

He loved the idea of isolation, embracing the hermit lifestyle.

Do you, though?

There was still a small part of him that longed for the family, the love, his mother had provided him. His father might have never been around, but when his mother had been alive, he'd felt part of a family. She'd brought light to his otherwise lonely life.

He missed her. It was a constant ache inside him. One he had learned to live with.

But after what happened with Kathleen, he wasn't going to risk opening his heart again, and there was no point mourning what he'd never had.

It's not meant to be.

He shook the thought away.

Thinking about things that wouldn't happen was distracting him from his task. He grabbed his hat and slammed it on his head, pulling the brim down. Then he pulled out the life jackets and tossed her one.

"Life jackets?" Lacey asked, confused.

He nodded. "It's part of the safety protocol. Put it on. We'll guide the passengers we're in charge of managing to do the same."

She nodded and put the life jacket on.

"Come on," he said gruffly. "Just follow my lead and you'll be fine."

He walked away from her swiftly, wanting to put some distance between them, but knowing that he couldn't completely leave her behind. She needed to know what to do, and this would help him gauge how she worked on the fly. Not that they got many traumatic injuries on a cruise.

Mostly it was people getting seasick or indigestion, or minor scrapes and injuries from people being a little too adventurous during a shore excursion.

Still, he wanted to see how she did.

Lacey kept up with him as he guided her out onto the deck, where the first officer was explaining the protocol over the speaker system. Thatcher stood on one side of the door, and Lacey took the position across from him.

Lacey didn't need much guidance, which he was impressed with. He closed the doors after everyone was on the deck and was standing in their assigned section.

"Now what?" she asked.

"We stand on the deck, and the ship pulls out. After we clear the port, everyone is free to go. We'll head back to the clinic, and I'll familiarize you with the layout and how I like things."

"Okay."

They stood side by side in the crowd of passengers and other crew members, and Thatcher was suddenly aware of how close she was. He could smell her hair, and it made his stomach knot. It smelled sweet, like honey, just like its color.

What is happening to you, Thatcher? Seriously, man. Get a grip.

It was not like him to wax poetic. What was happening to him? The ship lurched as it began to pull away, and before he could stop himself, he instinctively reached out and caught her, holding her tightly in his arms. He could feel the soft skin on her arms and looked down at her, her big blue eyes looking up at him in surprise and her lips just inches from his.

Big, soft, pink lips that he had the sudden urge to kiss.

Pink tinged her cheeks in embarrassment. "Thanks. I guess I don't have my sea legs yet."

"Not quite," he said gruffly.

Even though he knew that he should let go of her, he couldn't. He just held her there, pressed against him, the life vests the only thing separating them.

The rest of the crowd dispersed, and still he held on to her as they pulled out of Vancouver, heading north up the inside passage toward Alaska.

"I think I'm okay now," she whispered finally, pushing herself away from him.

"Right." He cleared his throat and let her go,

taking a step back. What was it about her? Why did he forget himself around her? From the moment he'd met her, when she was standing there in that wedding dress and he felt like it was some kind of weird sign, he'd been drawn to her.

He couldn't stop thinking about her and wondering why she hadn't got married. What had brought her here?

The idea of her being hurt made him feel protective, the same way he'd felt when his mother had been weak, vulnerable and sick.

And then he remembered that it really wasn't his business. Lacey was a stranger. She was his colleague, that was all. Letting someone—and especially letting Lacey—get too close to him was dangerous. If she got too close, she might discover who he really was. And if she found that out, who was to say others wouldn't also soon discover the truth?

He didn't want everyone to know that he was heir to the Duke of Weymouth. That he would have a seat in the House of Lords, that he had a duty pressing down on him like a thousand-pound weight.

He wasn't like his father. His father relished being the Duke of Weymouth and the attention it drew. The title meant nothing to Thatcher, and he didn't like the attention that came with it. And though his father might have been happy to put his title and duties before his family, Thatcher could never be like that.

His father had not understood why Thatcher didn't want the title, why Thatcher hated the limelight. They'd had so many bitter fights over their differences, leading up to their falling out.

"Come on," he said, breaking the silence that had settled between them. "Let's head back to the clinic so I can show you around."

Lacey nodded. "That sounds great."

They had just turned to walk back to the clinic when an ear-piercing scream stopped them in their tracks.

Thatcher turned around in time to see one of the passengers from the upper deck dangling over the railing before crashing down onto the deck he and Lacey were standing on.

CHAPTER THREE

LACEY HAD HEARD stories of people falling overboard, and there had been a few movies, usually ridiculous comedies, where a character fell from a ship into the ocean and had spiritual revelations with sea life, like dolphins, but she'd never thought she would witness someone falling onto the deck. Especially not on her first day.

Thatcher looked as shocked as she knew she did, so maybe he wasn't used to it either.

"Get a gurney," he shouted to one of the porters who was nearby.

"Should I go?" Lacey asked.

"No. They know where the emergency medical supplies are. You don't. I need your help here."

Lacey nodded and crouched down next to the unconscious man.

"Sir?" Thatcher asked as he began to go over the ABC's of triage. Airway, breathing and, well, they didn't really need to assess his consciousness level as he was obviously *un*conscious. "Sir, can you hear me?"

A porter appeared beside them with a first aid kit. Thatcher cracked it open and pulled on gloves, tossing a pair to Lacey as well.

"Sir, this is Dr. Bell. Can you hear me?" Thatcher asked again.

The man moaned.

"Pupils are reactive," Lacey said. "And he doesn't appear to have any contusions to the back of his head."

"It was lucky he didn't have that far to fall. Still can't rule out a head contusion. He did hit the deck hard," Thatcher muttered.

"What happened?" the man asked, beginning to regain consciousness. "Where am I?"

"On the *Alaskan Princess*. You fell from the upper deck," Lacey said.

"What?" the man asked.

"Harvey?" a frantic woman screeched as she rushed over to where they were crouched over their patient. "Oh, Harvey!"

"Is this your husband?" Thatcher asked.

"Yes. I'm his wife, June." June was frantic, and Lacey knew that she had to help calm her down so that Thatcher could get to work ascertaining what was wrong with Harvey. At least they had a name for him now.

"June, I'm Lacey. Can you tell me what happened? Did he faint before he fell?"

June nodded, but her gaze was still locked on her husband. "He'd been feeling a bit under the weather, but he still wanted to go on this trip, you know? It's been his lifelong dream."

"He wasn't feeling well?" Lacey asked.

"Right, but no fever. Just a bit dizzy, and I thought it might be excitement. We had a long flight yesterday from St. John's. That's in Newfoundland."

Lacey smiled. "Yes."

"Some people think we're from New Brunswick when I say that," June said, evidently on the edge of beginning to ramble—the last thing that Lacey needed right now.

"June, I need you to focus. He was dizzy, right?"

June nodded. "He was leaning over the side and waving. Then he just kind of slumped, and before I could catch him, he slipped over."

"Could be almost anything," Thatcher said, joining the conversation. "We'll get him on a backboard, take him down to the infirmary and run some tests."

Lacey nodded. "We'll figure out what's going on with Harvey," she said as reassuringly as she could.

June nodded nervously, wringing her hands.

Lacey went back to help Thatcher and the porters.

"Harvey, we're going to strap you to this backboard. Try not to move too much until I can properly examine you," Thatcher said.

Harvey nodded slowly.

The ship's infirmary looked well stocked from the brief glance that Lacey had managed the couple of times she'd been in there, but hopefully Harvey passed out and went over the side of the balcony for a simple reason.

Thankfully, he'd landed near them, and it wasn't a big drop down from the deck above.

She caught Thatcher watching her briefly as they worked together to get Harvey strapped down on the backboard, and her cheeks heated as she thought about being in his arms and how it would affect her.

It unnerved her how safe that short embrace had made her feel. His arms had been so strong, and for a moment she'd forgotten where she was and just let him hold her. She'd certainly never felt that way in Will's arms. Not that they had ever been particularly affectionate.

Thatcher made her feel like everything would be okay. She didn't know why, but Thatcher's strong arms around her grounded her.

For the first time since she'd arrived, she had

relaxed and found she hadn't wanted him to let go.

Then she'd remembered where she was. She had to remind herself that what she'd felt in that moment when she stumbled and fell into Thatcher's arms was nothing.

Today was an unusual day. She was dealing with the fresh hurt of having been burned by Will and Beth and run away from her wedding. Her nerves were all over the place, and she'd just been caught off guard when Thatcher's arms came around her.

That's all it was, and she had to hold on to that fact.

She didn't know Dr. Thatcher Bell well enough to feel anything for him.

She was just glad that he was there to catch her in that moment she'd stumbled.

Lacey was hoping for a quiet first day so she could continue to process everything that had happened to her in the last couple of hours, but obviously that was not meant to be, if medical cases were literally falling from the sky.

They got Harvey into the infirmary and onto the exam table in one of the small rooms, while June hovered nervously outside. The porters left and took the first aid kit and backboard to the spot on deck where they were stashed for emergencies such as that.

"What should we do first?" Lacey asked.

"We need to start an IV. I think Harvey is a bit dehydrated, and by the scent of booze on his breath, he might be intoxicated. First, though, I want to hook him up to an EKG and monitor his blood pressure for the next hour." Thatcher strung his stethoscope around his neck. "If you could tell his wife—"

"June," Lacey interjected.

"Yes, June. Please tell her she should return to her cabin as we don't have a waiting room here, and we'll have her paged when we're ready to let him go."

Lacey nodded and sent June on her way before collecting what was needed to start an intravenous line of fluids.

When she re-entered the small exam room, Thatcher was taking Harvey's blood pressure.

"So, you had a bit to drink today?" Thatcher asked.

"Yes. I was a wee bit nervous, you see," Harvey said sheepishly. "We landed yesterday. We had some oysters down at this seafood place, and the beer was mighty fine. I've never had a problem with seafood before. I'm from Newfoundland and my dad jigged cod for a living."

"Where did you have the oysters?" Lacey asked.

"O'Shanty's," Harvey responded.

Lacey made a face, which Thatcher saw but Harvey didn't as he'd closed his eyes and lay back.

Thatcher motioned for her to step out of the exam room.

"You reacted when the patient said O'Shanty's. Are you familiar with it?" he asked.

"Yes. I wouldn't eat anything there if you paid me a thousand dollars. It's notoriously cheap, but it's also notoriously dirty, and I can only imagine what the oysters would be like. We had a lot of cases of norovirus and hepatitis A come through the emergency room doors, and they were often tourists who'd had a seafood meal at O'Shanty's."

"No locals?"

"The odd one, but most people in Vancouver know to steer clear of O'Shanty's food menu."

Thatcher's lips pursed. "And what is the standard course of treatment for norovirus?"

Lacey tried not to be annoyed. She was used to doctors testing new-to-them nurses like this, so she went along with it.

"It's like any kind of stomach flu. It has to run its course. I didn't notice any jaundice, but we should check to make sure he's had his hepatitis A vaccination. It's too soon to tell if it's that, and I doubt it's vibrio, but it's something to mindful of."

Thatcher raised his eyebrows and smiled. "Well, let's hook him up to an IV and get him some fluids and get the EKG done to check his heart, just in case. I'll report to the captain what happened."

"Of course, Dr. Bell."

Thatcher walked away, and Lacey couldn't help but smile as she watched him. He might be a grump, and she might be strangely drawn to him, but he wasn't going to be hard to work with.

In fact, she was suddenly looking forward to her professional relationship with him. Because that was all she wanted from him.

Liar.

There was a part of her that did want something more. Something physical and primal.

Something intense she'd never felt before.

It was unnerving.

Thatcher made his way up to the bridge to officially report what happened to the captain, though he was sure that the captain would already know someone had fallen over a balcony. Thankfully, the patient was stable and didn't seem to have any fractures. He likely had a mild concussion, though, so some rest would be in order over the next few days while the ship was at sea before they reached their first port.

He dashed up the stairs and entered the main

bridge area, which was full of computers and other high-tech nautical equipment, and found Captain Aldridge was at the helm. He turned and looked back at him.

"Ah, Dr. Bell. I heard there was quite the excitement when we were leaving port."

Thatcher saluted and nodded. "Indeed. We had a gentleman faint and fall over a balcony, dropping about ten feet from one deck to another."

"And how is he?"

"He's stable. There were no fractures, but he was quite dizzy, so my nurse and I are monitoring him and trying to ascertain what might have caused him to faint in the first place."

The captain nodded. "I'm glad to hear that he wasn't more seriously hurt and that we don't need to call for an air ambulance to come and remove him from the ship."

"Yes, he was lucky," Thatcher responded.

"Incidentally, how is your new nurse working out?" Captain Aldridge asked. "I'm very glad she was able to come on board at the last minute, even if she was a bit overdressed for the job."

Thatcher chuckled. "Nurse Greenwood is working out quite fine."

"I'll say," the first mate interjected with a snicker.

"Have you even met her?" Thatcher snapped.

"No, but I did see her briefly when she came on board."

Thatcher wasn't the biggest fan of the first officer, Matt Bain, because he didn't like that he was such a cad. His own father had been a bit of a playboy, and Thatcher remembered how much it had hurt his mother.

Matt's interest in Lacey set him on edge.

Why is it bothering you? It's not your business.

"Nurse Greenwood and I will be quite busy on this voyage," Thatcher said stiffly, changing the topic.

The captain looked confused. "Busy? I hope not. I don't want this voyage to be one of the damned, Dr. Bell."

Thatcher smiled. "What I meant is, there's a lot to show her, and she's eager to learn."

Matt sniggered. "I'll bet."

Thatcher glared and clenched his fists.

Captain Aldridge glanced back at Matt and then at Thatcher. "Well, I'll leave you both to it. Keep me updated on the passenger's prognosis or if there's anything they need. I plan to go down and speak to him later."

"I will, Captain. Thank you." Thatcher saluted again and left the bridge.

It had taken every ounce of strength he had not to leap across the bridge and knock that smirk off Matt's face. And he was annoyed because it had to do with Lacey. Why did she bring out this protective side in him?

It's because she's vulnerable. She's a runaway bride.

Still, he didn't know the circumstances of what had brought her on board. So what was it about her that had him ruffled?

He remembered when he'd first met Kathleen. She'd been hurt and vulnerable.

Maybe he just had a soft spot for women who seemed to need him. He'd watched his mother be treated terribly by his father, her heart breaking over and over again, and though Thatcher's heart had ached, he'd been a child, and there was nothing he could've done then. As a man, he vowed to be different.

He wanted to cherish and protect women, but he'd been duped by Kathleen and others before her. They only wanted his title and his money— never him—and so those women had moved on to someone else. It's why he didn't get involved seriously with anyone anymore.

Medicine and saving lives, helping others, were honorable, and what he'd always wanted to do, so that was what he'd focused on these last few years.

But here he was, falling into that trap again, feeling like he needed to protect Lacey.

Well, he could keep her busy so Matt didn't bother her, but he'd keep his distance.

He wasn't going to put his heart on the line again.

Even if you want to?

Yes, there was a part of him that wanted a family and kids, and he hated that Lacey brought those thoughts to the surface. He was going to have to do his best to keep away from her so he didn't get trapped in her snare. Not that Lacey was consciously trying to trap him, but there was something about her that drew him in like a moth to a flame.

Lacey made sure that Harvey was settled and the fluids and antibiotics were running. She didn't want to take the chance that it could be something like vibrio, though it was a rare infection and if it was caught early, it didn't do as much damage. Thankfully, Harvey had his hepatitis A vaccination last year, so they didn't have to worry about liver damage.

When she closed the door to the exam room, where Harvey was stable and napping, she ran smack-dab into Thatcher, who looked a bit flustered and annoyed.

There was a strange energy coming off him. He was agitated.

"Is everything okay, Dr. Bell?" she asked cautiously.

"I told you, you can call me Thatcher," he said. "And yes. I was just up on the bridge letting the captain know that the patient was stable. How is Harvey?"

"He's doing well. Blood pressure is stable now he's getting some fluids, and I started him on an antibiotic, just in case it's more than food poisoning."

Thatcher nodded and crossed his arms. "And his EKG?"

"Normal."

"Good."

"He may have a mild concussion, but we'll continue to monitor him to be sure."

"I was thinking the same thing. He may have landed feet first like a cat, but he still could have banged his head on the way down. Did you check his legs?"

"No fractures, no swelling. There's some bruising, but nothing alarming. I think that once his course of antibiotics and saline bag is empty, we can send him back to his cabin. He'll need a light diet of crackers and broth for the next couple of days and, to be safe, no seafood or alcohol."

Thatcher smiled briefly. "I agree. You did a good job out there today, Lacey. I was quite impressed with how you jumped right into the fray."

"I'm used to triage situations as I've been a nurse practitioner for some time. I'm not fresh out of school."

"Of course. Still, sometimes in a new job, there's uncertainty, even if you've done the very same thing many times before. And that was certainly an unusual situation."

"You've never had a man fall from one of the decks?"

He smiled, and it went straight to his eyes. It made her feel warm. She liked this smile on him. It was genuine and friendly. Will was all business and never smiled. He didn't have the best bedside manner with his patients.

Thatcher might try to act like a grump, but he had real empathy, and that empathy made her heart skip a beat.

Get a grip, Lacey.

It was not the time to think like this. She'd just gotten out of an obviously bad relationship. The last thing she needed was to have the hots for her new boss.

"I have, but it's not quite the same, and it's never happened right when we left port. That was a first," he said, interrupting her thoughts.

She chuckled. "Well, I guess fate decided to really test me tonight."

An uneasy silence fell between them. Her pulse was racing, and she didn't know what it was about being around him that made her feel this way—uneasy, but not afraid.

It was something else. Something she had never quite felt before.

A feeling she didn't know existed.

That instant animal attraction.

Like she'd been hit with a magnetic bolt.

Her cheeks heated, and she cleared her throat. "Well, I better get rid of this medical waste."

"Right, right," he said nervously. "I'll go check on him. You've had quite the day, so after you clean up, why don't you take the rest of the night off? Get something to eat and rest. I'll expect to see you at zero five hundred hours tomorrow."

"Who covers the night?"

"There's a call button for me. Usually the night is quiet."

"Don't say that," she teased.

"What?"

"Never say it's going to be quiet." She knocked on a wooden doorjamb. "You say that in the emergency room, and inevitably things go wonky."

"It's been a long time since I worked in A&E. I don't remember all the superstitions."

"You don't have superstitions in England?"

"Perhaps, but I don't recall much about my

short stint in A&E. I had a private practice on Harley Street."

"Wow, Harley Street. That's quite posh, isn't it? Did you treat any members of the royal family?"

A strange expression crossed his face then.

"Yes. Why this sudden interest in my past?"

"Why the sudden interest in mine earlier?" she clapped back.

"You're new here. I'm not." He got up and walked away from her.

She sighed and collected the medical waste to take down to the incinerator chute. Even though she wasn't tired, she was going to accept his offer and take the rest of the night off.

She still couldn't shake the feeling that she'd seen him somewhere before.

Does it matter?

She realized it didn't. All that mattered was that they kept a good working relationship. There weren't many places to hide on a cruise ship, so whether she liked it or not, they were stuck together for the next month.

CHAPTER FOUR

Lacey tossed and turned all night as rain pattered against the porthole in her room. The ship was rocking back and forth, and she wasn't used to the motion of the waves.

They were sailing up what she'd heard one of the crew refer to as "the inside passage" and knew it wouldn't be as rough as the open sea they'd encounter when they headed further up the coast of Alaska toward the Bering Sea. She needed to prepare herself for the choppier waters still to come.

She also couldn't sleep because she couldn't get Thatcher out of her mind. All she could think about was his arms around her and how safe his embrace had made her feel.

It bothered her.

Only twenty-four hours ago, she was on the edge of getting married, looking forward to stability at last. Instead, her sense of security had been shattered, and now she was on a cruise ship, of all places, trying to clear her head of indecent thoughts about her new boss.

Her stomach twisted in a knot.

What was wrong with her?

Why didn't Will's betrayal affect her more? Why wasn't she crying over him?

Why did she only have thoughts for Thatcher, a man she'd just met?

The phone in her quarters rang, and she reached over to grab it, hoping she didn't groan too much when she answered it.

"Greenwood speaking," she said groggily.

"I didn't wake you, did I?" Thatcher said on the other end of the line.

"No. I wasn't sleeping well." She glanced over at the clock and saw it was two in the morning.

"We've had an influx of seasickness, and I'm hoping that you can come and assist me."

"I'll be right there."

"Thank you."

Lacey hung up the phone and grabbed her scrubs. She might not be able to sleep, and she might be thinking about Thatcher and how he made her heart beat a bit faster when she shouldn't, but at least she could throw herself into her job and forget about all this.

She quickly got ready, tied back her hair, made sure her face was clean and headed straight up to the infirmary.

As she stepped out into the hall, she ran into someone.

"Whoa," the man said, his arms around her.

"I'm so sorry." She glanced up and saw from his uniform that he was one of the crew members from the bridge.

"I'm the first officer, Matthew Bain," he said, smiling. "You can call me Matt."

"Right. I'm Nurse Greenwood." She tried to step back so she could continue down the hall, but he stood in her way, blocking her. "Look, I'm sorry, but…"

"No need to be sorry. Where are you off to in such a rush?" he asked.

"The infirmary. There are a few sick passengers, so if you don't mind…"

"I can walk you there."

She groaned inwardly. This guy couldn't take a hint, could he?

"It's kind of you to offer, but you don't have to."

"I know I don't have to, but it would be my pleasure."

She smiled, but it was forced. "Fine."

She hoped that he would get the hint to leave her alone as she quickly walked down the hall toward the staff stairwells, but instead he followed her.

"You're in quite a rush. It's just seasickness."

"And the doctor is overwhelmed," she said over her shoulder. "It's the middle of the night. I'm not going to leave him in the lurch."

Lacey dashed up the stairs, but Matt kept pace beside her.

"There's not much to do for seasickness. The problem is the passage is choppy. There are some storms, but nothing this ship can't handle, so don't worry."

"I wasn't worried." She stopped in front of the infirmary. "I better go and help the doctor. Thanks for walking with me. Sorry I can't stay and chat more."

He stepped in front of her. "Would you like to meet for a drink tomorrow? There's a great eighties-themed bar on deck twenty. It's a lot of fun."

She was about to turn him down when the door opened and a tired-looking Thatcher peered out. The moment his gaze landed on Matt, his body tensed and his eyes narrowed.

"If you could pull yourself away from flirting, I could really use your help, Nurse Greenwood."

Her cheeks flushed with embarrassment and anger.

"Relax, Dr. Bell. I was just escorting Nurse Greenwood here," Matt said.

She rolled her eyes. "Excuse me."

She pushed past Thatcher and went about

getting medicine ready. She assumed that they would visit the passengers' cabins and administer the anti-nausea drugs there.

Lacey really didn't know what was going on in the hallway between Matt and Thatcher, but she also really didn't care.

The door shut, and Thatcher came over to help pack the bags, but said nothing. She could feel that he was annoyed.

"What is wrong with you?" she snapped.

"There's nothing wrong with me. I'm focusing on my work. Unlike some people, I know that's more important than flirting," he said coldly.

"What?" she said in disbelief. "I wasn't flirting."

"Everyone fawns over Matt."

"Well, I'm not everyone."

"I'm sure."

Lacey rolled her eyes. "I was trying to get rid of him. I accidentally bumped into him in the hall and he insisted on following me here. I was almost running and he jogged beside me."

Thatcher snorted, and a smile tugged at the corners of his lips. "Really?"

"Yes. He couldn't quite take the hint that I would not be interested in accompanying him for a drink at an eighties-themed bar."

"Well, it is a fun bar. They have karaoke, and there's lots of neon," Thatcher teased.

"Are we really going to talk about neon at two in the morning?" she asked, laughing softly as the tension that had been hovering between them melted away.

Which was a relief. It was her emotions running amok given what an unusual day it had been.

In the light of the infirmary, with patients to attend to and work to do, she relaxed.

All she wanted to do was work.

And it was easy to work with Thatcher...so far.

She glanced over at him prepping the bags with medicine, and she felt that rush, that zing, traveling through her body again.

A flush crept over her skin.

What is going on?

She ignored that thought and focused on prepping her kit.

"I'll take the more severe cases, so here's your list of patients. Give them an injection, and leave them with some anti-nausea tablets. You know the drill, I'm sure."

Lacey nodded. "I do."

"Hopefully they'll feel better when the weather improves."

"Let me guess. This hasn't happened before to this extent?"

Thatcher chuckled. "Only once, on the second voyage I did. It happens more when we're closer to the Bering Sea. The inside passage is smooth…usually."

"It's because you said it was going to be quiet," she teased.

He groaned. "I certainly hope word doesn't get out, or people will be calling to put Weymouth's head on a pike—" He stopped himself and clammed up, looking annoyed with himself.

"Who is Weymouth?"

"The town I come from."

"I thought you came from London?" she asked.

"I worked in London, but I was born in Weymouth. Does it matter?"

"It's just that the name rings a bell. My mother is a huge royal follower, so I know that a few years ago, the heir to the Duke of Weymouth just up and left. No one knows where he went. She's read a lot of conspiracy theories about what might have happened."

Something was niggling at her as Thatcher locked up the infirmary, his whole body tense.

"Does she really? Well, I don't know much about the Duke of Weymouth. Like I said, I was born there, and that's about it," he stated.

They walked in silence down the hall and up the stairs. At the deck where she would begin seeing patients, he paused.

"When you're done, report back to the infirmary, and we can go over the roster for the day. I think we'll be done just as our day starts."

"Of course."

She watched as he climbed the steps. What was with him? He ran so hot and cold, she was going to get whiplash if she wasn't careful.

He was kicking himself internally as he attended to the more severe cases of seasickness and one case of what appeared to be morning sickness, which was a first for him on this cruise too.

He made a note in that patient's chart to have Lacey follow up with the soon-to-be mother.

Thatcher had made a huge mistake when he'd been joking with Lacey and referred to himself as Weymouth. It had been quite some time since he'd done that. Usually no one got it if he let something like that slip, but of course Lacey's mother had to be a royal watcher.

He knew that there were various conspiracy theories about his disappearance, but he didn't want his family correcting what was written in the press and feeding the beast. Thatcher just wanted to be left alone.

Over the years that he'd been working on these cruises and spending his vacation time in Canada, he'd had a few close calls, but he always managed to evade the reporters and photographers.

There was no love lost between Thatcher and the papers. They had plastered his name everywhere when Kathleen left him for another man and showcased his father's extramarital affairs throughout his childhood. He could still perfectly picture the hurt etched on his mother's face whenever she saw the images.

He hated that he had no privacy at home.

It was different here. Here he was anonymous.

Until he'd said the name Weymouth and she'd caught him on his slip.

He had to be more careful. The problem was, he let his guard down around Lacey. It was so easy to talk to her, and he didn't know why.

Maybe because you're lonely?

Thatcher shook that thought away. He had to regain control.

He finished his house calls to the passengers just as the sun was coming up and made his way back down to the infirmary to find Lacey sitting outside the door. He realized she didn't have a set of keys yet. He'd have to make sure she got them soon.

"Sorry," he said quickly. "Were you waiting long?"

"No. I just got here." She stood up.

"I have a pregnant patient for you to follow

up on. She just found out." Thatcher handed her the file.

"Oh, how lovely." Lacey flipped through it. "I'll check on her later. If she has extreme morning sickness, I want to make sure she gets enough fluids. Although the weather has turned nicer. I did see the sun through the clouds."

"Yes. It should be a calmer day." He opened the door, and they set their gear down and cleaned up. "Would you like to go get some coffee with me? I'm sure one of the coffee shops on the main deck will be open, and I think we'll need it."

"Yes. I would love that."

Thatcher locked up and posted a sign with his pager number in case anyone needed them. Then they made their way to the main deck.

It was still early in the morning, and most of the passengers were still sleeping, but there were a few milling around as they made their way through the main deck to the upper decks of the ship. The main deck wasn't open to the elements as it would have been on a warm Caribbean cruise. Instead there were domed windows to allow the sunlight in and heat up where everyone congregated, so it felt like you were on a tropical cruise.

There were several couples walking or running the perimeter of the deck—the early bird passengers getting in their exercise as the ship started to come to life for its very first full day at sea.

"Is this your first time on a cruise?" Thatcher asked, trying to make small talk as they stood in the short line for coffee.

"It is. I've always wanted to do something like this. When I was a kid, the most exciting moves were when my father would get postings in the far north. Exciting, but scary. I didn't always enjoy moving around."

"Was your father in the armed forces?"

"No, he was an officer with the Royal Canadian Mounted Police—one of the few officers that ended up finishing off his career in Ottawa, protecting the prime minister. When I was a little girl, he had several postings in the Northwest Territories and Nunavut."

"Did you ever live in the Yukon?"

"Yes." She smiled. "And he had a short posting in Inuvik. That was before the road was built to Tuktoyaktuk. We only lived there for six months. Never got to really experience a winter up that far, but it was still one of my favorite places. It was adventurous."

He smiled and nodded. That adventure was something he'd always craved when he was younger, which was why he was here and why he wanted to stay. He was envious of her childhood. It was so unlike his.

"That sounds like a lot of fun."

"Well, it's just Canada, and when I became older and started traveling on my own, I did a bit of the United States, but I haven't been anywhere truly exciting like Europe or Australia."

"Europe is great, but it's crowded."

"What's wrong with crowds?"

"I like space."

"You're on a cruise ship. There isn't exactly a lot of space here."

"This is only temporary. In fact, this is my last trip. I'll finally have enough."

Her finely arched eyebrows rose, and her blue eyes lit up. "Oh? You'll have enough for what?"

"A piece of land in the Yukon. Preferably near Dawson, somewhere in the mountains." It would be his own land, land he'd worked hard to be able to afford, with no help from his father or the family fortune.

"That sounds wonderful. Are you going to continue practicing medicine?"

"Yes. That's the plan." He ordered them two coffees—free, because they were staff—and they wandered away from the shop and found a couple of chairs out in the sunlight, where it was warm.

He was actually shocked that he'd told her his

plan. It was something that he'd kept to himself for so long. The only other person he'd told was Kathleen, and she'd wrinkled her nose in distaste.

"Why would you want to do that?" she'd asked.

"Because it's exciting! Don't you want to have this kind of a chance at something new?"

She'd smiled placatingly. *"Yes, but not in the Yukon. I was thinking more of Majorca or somewhere in the Mediterranean, and just for trips. I don't mind taking trips, but to somewhere trendy and fashionable. I mean, you are in line to the British throne."*

"A lot of people would have to die for me to become king," he'd said dryly. *"And that's something I would never want. I'm not even sure I want to be duke when my father dies."*

She'd looked horrified. *"What? You can't turn down the title."*

"Why not? My brother, Michael, would be an excellent duke. He's more interested in the land and more involved with Parliament. I want to be a doctor, out in the wilds somewhere, helping people and living an adventure."

His father would never agree to it, but with Kathleen at his side, he wouldn't care. They'd make it work.

"I'm sure you'll get over it. You'll spend a

week there and you'll change your mind and see sense."

She'd patted his head like he was some kind of petulant child and left.

And still he hadn't seen sense and realized that Kathleen wasn't the one for him.

He'd been so blinded by her beauty and the fact that she kept saying she loved him. And then, when he told her that he was serious about his plans for the Yukon, she'd cheated on him with a wealthier man. One who ran in all the right circles and didn't mind the press. It was demoralizing. Broke his heart, embarrassed him.

It was obvious to Thatcher the people that operated in his father's realm didn't quite get his passion and would never understand him.

It was better to leave. Maybe then his father would stop insisting he take the title.

Which was why he was here. And now he was so close to having everything he'd ever wanted.

Not everything.

Thatcher shook that thought away. He wouldn't think of his lost dreams of family or of a wife.

"Well," she said, "I think the two places out of Canada I would most like to go to are Iceland and Antarctica."

"You really do like the cold then, don't you?" he teased.

"I do. There's just something about the north."

She sighed sadly. "I wanted to work in Iqaluit or even further north, in a place like Alert, in Nunavut, but my fiancé, or rather my ex-fiancé, didn't want to go that far. So I stayed in Vancouver."

He got the sense that she hadn't been happy. It was at that moment that he thought maybe he'd pegged her wrong, and he was annoyed at himself for judging her so quickly.

"Is that why you left?" he asked gently. "I know you said you didn't want to talk about why you arrived here in your wedding dress..."

"No, it's fine. Yes, I ran from him. I caught him in the act with my maid of honor."

"Ah." He winced. "I'm sorry."

She shrugged. "It is what it is. I realized as I watched him with my former best friend that I wasn't that hurt that he was cheating on me. I guess part of me expected it since I don't have the best luck with men." Her cheeks flushed pink. "And I don't know why I'm telling you this."

"It's okay, but why marry him if you expected him to cheat?" Thatcher asked.

Lacey shrugged and picked at the corner of the napkin on the table. "It seemed like the logical thing to do at the time. It was safe, or so I thought. I left the church after I caught him in the act, as it were. We both got ready at the church. I thought he'd be alone, and he was not."

"And you don't regret walking out?" he asked.

"Not so far, but it has been exceptionally busy!" She laughed, and he couldn't help but laugh with her.

It was easy to laugh with her.

And that thought scared him. He stared at his empty coffee cup. "Well, we better go and plan out the roster for the day. You know, you should try a couple of the shore excursions if you get the chance."

"I'd like to. I'm very excited that we're going to stop in Skagway. I've always wanted to explore that city. Maybe there will even be time to take the train into the Yukon up the White Pass. That's also on the bucket list."

"I think time can be made for that." He smiled and stood up.

Lacey followed.

They tossed their coffee cups in the trash and walked in silence back to the infirmary. It had been a long time since he sat down and really talked to someone.

It was nice, but he had to remind himself to be careful.

He didn't want to get hurt again, and he didn't want Lacey to be hurt either.

At the end of this cruise, he was going to buy

CHAPTER FIVE

LACEY QUICKLY FELL into a routine on ship as the rough weather settled down and time at sea became more peaceful. She made her rounds to check on those patients who had extreme seasickness that first night and checked in on Harvey, who was recovering well from his food poisoning and minor concussion.

Everything was going really smoothly, and she appreciated that it kept her busy. Busy was good because it meant she didn't have to think about Will or Beth or her failed attempt at marriage.

It was nice to focus just on the work…and Thatcher.

But thinking about Thatcher and how much she'd enjoyed working with him over the past couple of days was distracting.

Lacey tried to keep her distance, but it was hard to do that in a small infirmary, and every time she tried to keep herself occupied with

his land in the Yukon and start his local practice. There was no stopping him.

He was going to follow through.

And nothing was going to change his mind.

busywork and admin, she'd see emails from Will and Beth in her inbox.

Lacey couldn't bring herself to face the emails. She was mad at herself for being duped and mad at herself for agreeing to marry Will, for not seeing the signs earlier. She didn't need to read some half-hearted explanation of why he'd cheated when she should have known all along that it wasn't to be.

Work always came first for Will. They never talked at the hospital unless they had a brief moment, and then it was quick and to the point.

When she talked to Thatcher, it was different. Easier. But since their coffee a couple of days ago, he himself was acting a bit distant, as if he was keeping her at arm's length. And even though she shouldn't be bothered because she was only here to work, she found she was sad.

You can't get attached.

She wasn't looking for love.

Only a lucky few could find love.

She wasn't one of them.

Maybe it was for the best that he kept his distance, making it easier for her to fight this strange, overpowering attraction that she was feeling for him. When she was around him, she felt able to let go. Usually she was pretty private, but around him, her pulse would race and all those things she kept close to her heart just came pouring out.

It was like she lost all sense around him.

She saw him every day, but Lacey missed chatting with him, like they had the first day of the voyage. It was better that they were professional, but she liked talking with him, and she liked learning more about him. He was so sure about his plans. So focused.

Lacey was a bit envious of that. He had a solid plan for the future, whereas she wasn't sure where she was going. She had learned to roll with the punches and pick up and move wherever her dad got a new posting, but there was always a part of her that longed for roots. Now, once again, she didn't know what she would do next.

She craved having a place to belong, like she did when they lived in Yellowknife. When she'd been her happiest.

You could go back.

It wasn't the first time she'd had the thought, but Carol was gone now.

The people she once knew there were probably gone. It was no longer home.

A lump formed in her throat, and Lacey shook the thought away. This was why she tried to never let herself think of Yellowknife or the fact Carol was gone.

She finished up writing in her patients' charts

and started wrapping everything up. She was off duty soon, and she thought she might take advantage of the chance to take a shore excursion—a small boat trip inland and then a kayak journey to an inlet to see grizzlies in a hidden bay. Seeing grizzlies sounded like an experience she shouldn't miss. Of course, she wasn't here to have a vacation—she was here to work and keep her mind off the things she didn't want to think about—but that didn't mean she couldn't also have a bit of fun in her downtime.

"You're off duty soon, aren't you?" Thatcher asked from his office.

She turned and looked back through his open door. "I am."

"What are you going to do?"

"I might do the shore excursion to see the grizzlies."

"I've done that one before. It's really good. You almost finished? The first boat leaves in an hour," Thatcher said, coming out of his office. She noticed that he was back in his officer's white uniform. She hadn't been able to see it when he was sitting behind his desk at his computer, and she couldn't help but admire how good he looked. She'd always had a thing for a man in uniform, and this one fit his muscular body like a glove.

Warmth crept up her cheeks, and she hoped

she wasn't blushing, which she always seemed to do when Thatcher was around. She felt like a young girl who had her first crush.

"Why are you so adamant I go now?" Lacey asked.

He smiled. "It's a once-in-a-lifetime experience."

"Okay. I'm almost done, though, and there are small boats leaving all day. I don't have to be on the very first boat."

"You know, I find the last boat out to the inlet is more magical. The water is so clear, and with the moon and stars, it's like a mirror."

"That's quite poetic," she teased.

He smiled briefly. "Well, I can be poetic when the mood strikes me. Which is not often."

She laughed softly. "That's a shame. You have quite the nice accent to take the stage at Stratford and recite Shakespeare."

"I am not an actor," he groused. "At Eton we often performed Shakespeare, and I didn't have an acting bone in my body. It was shameful. It would always make my father wince at how terrible I was."

"Eton? Wow, I had no idea. So did you go on to Cambridge or Oxford?"

He frowned and looked a bit worried. "Cambridge."

"Sorry, I didn't mean to pry. I know you don't like it when I pry."

"No." He shook his head. "No, it's not that. It's just I don't have very fond memories of my childhood, and I don't like talking about it. I prefer to focus on the future and the plans I'm looking forward to."

"I'm envious of your plans," she muttered, not really wanting to let it out, but unable to stop herself. She didn't know what was going to happen when she got back to Vancouver. All the plans she'd made for herself the last couple years were gone.

"Are you?" he asked, curious.

"See, my childhood was very transient, but happy. I love my parents." She smiled just thinking of them. They had always been there for her, and her father had been the one to help her when she'd run from her wedding.

"He did what?" her father had shouted.

"Don't shout, Dad. It's okay." She'd continued to sort out her suitcase. "I'm not upset. I mean, I am, but right now I've just got to focus on going away from here."

Her father had looked at her, concerned. "Going where?"

"Somewhere to think. I'm not sure I really believe in love, but I know that I don't believe in a relationship founded on unfaithfulness."

Her father had nodded. "You were always quite pragmatic and logical. I just want you to be safe. What do you need me to do?"

She'd hugged her father. "Move my stuff out of his place while I'm gone. I don't have much... you know I'm a minimalist."

Her father had grinned and touched her cheek. "And then?"

"I'll call the hospital and do what I have to, and quit my job. I just need to clear my head and figure out my next steps."

"The whole world is yours," her father had said gently. "I never thanked you for all those times we moved because of my job. I know it was always hard on you and your mother, but you two... I couldn't have done what I did if it wasn't for you and your mom."

She'd kissed her father on his cheek. "I'd be grateful if you could also explain my decision to Mom. I know she's a bit more emotional than us."

"I will. Just be safe."

Her parents were loving and supportive, and she was so thankful for that. She couldn't have done this—taken this leap—without their support and her father's help.

Her father had been right. The whole world was hers, but she didn't know where to go, and she was envious that Thatcher had this plan all thought out.

She wanted roots, but she didn't know where she wanted to live. The world was open, but also closed. It was scary. She felt like she was free-falling.

"I did not have such a tranquil childhood," he muttered. "I am glad you did, though, but don't be envious of me."

"Why not? You have plans. I don't."

He smiled at her. "You have a plan for today. You're going to take a boat up to the Khutzeymateen and see some grizzly bears."

She smiled. "Yes. I suppose I do have that plan."

"Just because it appears that someone has their life together doesn't mean that they do. In fact, they often don't." There was sadness in his voice.

Lacey didn't know what he meant by that, but the moment he said it, she could sense that he wasn't happy, and she couldn't figure out why. For one moment, she wanted to take him in her arms and reassure him that everything would be okay—making him feel safe the same way he had made her feel safe—but how could she comfort him when she wasn't even sure what she was comforting him for? She didn't even know him.

"You should go," Thatcher said. "Go enjoy the bears. It's amazing."

"Why are you trying to push me out the door?"

"I'm not. I'm trying to make sure you don't miss the chance of a lifetime. So go!"

Lacey closed her chart. "I swear I won't miss the chance of a lifetime."

Thatcher smiled the friendly, warm smile that made her heart skip a beat. It was so easy being around him. "Okay, see that you don't, and stop stressing."

Thatcher watched Lacey finish up her paperwork. He didn't know why she was envious of him. There was nothing to be envious about.

He might have plans, but it didn't mean his life was together. Sure, he liked to think he had it all figured out, but then something happened to prove him wrong. Something like his brother calling to let him know their father was seriously ill.

He felt lost.

His father had never been a true and loving father to him, but Thatcher felt bad to learn the duke was sick.

At least Lacey had a happy childhood.

He couldn't say that.

His father had been cruel. He didn't care about his wife or children and was never around, too busy cheating on his wife and breaking her heart over and over again. Thatcher's mother had been loving and caring, but also so sick, and he'd spent a lot of his childhood worried about her.

The only bright spot in his early years was his younger brother, Michael. They had been close once, but Michael had been so hurt when Thatcher walked away from it all, and their bond had been broken. He had never wanted to hurt Michael like that, and it pained him to have his brother angry at him, but Thatcher wanted nothing his father had to offer. He'd really had no choice but to walk away, but he always regretted leaving Michael behind.

Leaving Michael with their father.

But Thatcher had no choice. He had to leave, and he had to live out his dream. It was his life and he owed his father nothing.

Michael liked dealing with the estate and loved politics, but their father refused to let him take over, claiming it was Thatcher's birthright, not Michael's.

So he might have plans, but his life wasn't together yet.

Not in the slightest.

It wouldn't be until this cruise was over and he was moving up to the Yukon to scout out his piece of land and then slowly building his practice while he built his own house. That's what he wanted.

Everything had been so clear in his head. Thatcher knew exactly what he had to do, but now Michael was begging him to come home and make things right.

Thatcher couldn't. He was so close to having everything he wanted, and he just couldn't give it up, his future, couldn't walk away from it.

You walked away from the estate.

That thought made his stomach twist. The estate was a birthright not a commitment.

Medicine was his life. And what he'd wanted to do for so long.

And there was Lacey. The runaway bride who had shown up as his nurse.

He wanted to ignore her, but he was drawn to her.

No matter how many times he told himself that he was going to keep his distance and just remain professional, he couldn't. He would try to work, and he'd catch himself staring at her. She was beautiful, and being around her, he didn't feel so lonely.

She wasn't easy to ignore.

He was a moth and she was the flame.

Are you seriously comparing yourself to a bug right now?

Thatcher laughed at that thought.

He opened up his email and saw that his

brother had emailed him again, but he couldn't bring himself to open it.

Instead he glanced out the window of his office and saw Lacey was still there, charting. She hadn't left yet, and he couldn't help but smile when he saw her there.

She was supposed to be off duty and yet she was still working.

It was a quiet day, and she should take a chance to explore like most of the passengers who were off ship, enjoying the shore excursions.

He sighed. At least she was dedicated to her work—that was something to be admired. He opened up the door to his small office. He wouldn't mind her staying here with him all day, but she deserved time to enjoy herself too.

"Lacey, didn't I tell you to leave thirty minutes ago?"

"You did," she said, not looking up at him.

"Would you come in here please?"

She rolled her eyes, closed her chart and came into his office, her arms crossed and an annoyed look on her face.

"If you keep interrupting my work then I can't leave on the shore excursion at all," she stated.

"I'm beginning to suspect that's what you want. You don't know what you're missing." He motioned her to come closer. "I'm going to show you the photos I took when I went on the excursion a couple of years ago."

She rolled her eyes and came to stand beside him. The closer she got, the more he could smell the scent of her shampoo, and it fired his blood. This was the opposite of keeping his distance from her. He wasn't sure what he was doing or what possessed him, but he didn't care. He never showed these pictures to anyone, but right in this moment he wanted to share them with her. Which was strange. Anytime he showed Kathleen a glimpse of these secret dreams of life in the north, she'd whine or ignore him.

And his father had had no interest either.

Thatcher had always had to keep it private, but here was an opportunity to share it without the fear of judgment. The fact that it was Lacey he was sharing it with felt intimate and made his pulse race with anticipation. He wanted to reveal this piece of himself to her.

And her reaction would let him know if he was attracted to the wrong kind of woman again. Did she genuinely love the north or was she just saying she did?

Could she be lying or putting on an act the same way Kathleen did in the beginning of their relationship because she wanted the title of duchess?

Don't think about Kathleen.

"What am I looking at?" Lacey asked.

"The inlet, before you get to the floating lodge that some people travel to stay at."

"A floating lodge?" she asked, leaning over. A strand of her soft honey-blond hair escaped from her tight bun and tickled his neck.

He tried to shift and move away from her, only he couldn't without it seeming obvious that he wanted to put distance between them. So he focused on trying to ignore how close she was to him.

"That looks like an amazing place to stay! Do they get there by boat?"

"They can if it's a flat-bottom boat, but mostly people who stay at the floating lodge take a float plane from Prince Rupert. Our passengers, and you, if you hurry up, take a flat-bottom boat up the inlet, and the lodge provides kayaks for those who want to explore."

"Do you recommend the kayaking?"

"Yes." He clicked on the next picture, which showed some of the rain forest and the bears. Pictures that calmed him. It was experiences like this that had solidified his desire to live in the north.

There was peace here.

For so many years, it felt like his soul was

uneasy. Since his mother had died, he was dissatisfied and unhappy—restless. Thatcher had tried to fit into his father's world, but the more he tried to be like the man his father wanted him to be, the more he lost himself.

The more he hated himself.

Then he met Kathleen, and for that short time he was with her, he'd been happy.

He thought she wanted the same things he did. Only she hadn't.

Kathleen had lied to him, broken his heart.

And he'd made a promise to himself not to end up like his mother.

Sad.

Shattered.

Jaded.

Trapped in a loveless marriage.

Here, in nature, and up north, he was who he truly believed he should be.

"I guess I will do the kayak, then," Lacey said, interrupting his thoughts.

"You should. It was one of the best experiences of my time in this job."

She glanced over at him, her lips close to his, and his throat went dry. He could see her neck, slender and long, and he wanted to kiss it. To feel her pulse beneath his lips. His heart was racing, and his body stiffened. She was so close, he would feel her warmth, and he wanted to drown himself in her. To wrap his arms around her and take care of her.

"Doctor?" someone called out. He was relieved at the distraction of a patient.

Lacey started to leave his office, but he reached out and took her hand to stop her.

"You're off duty. I'll take care of this. You stay and look at the photos, convince yourself to go."

She smiled. "Fine."

He got up and left her. It was good to put some distance between them. And fast.

Lacey continued to scroll through the pictures. They were beautiful. She didn't know why she'd been debating going on a shore excursion. It was a great opportunity. It was a change. And maybe the change of scenery would help clear her head, give her the space she needed to process everything.

She really needed to do that.

So why did she feel like she didn't deserve it?

Because you're here to work, not enjoy yourself.

Except she was enjoying herself. She'd been on this cruise for several days, and she'd never enjoyed work this much before. Yes, she'd loved her job at the hospital, but the hospital stayed put. The cruise went somewhere new every day, and she never knew quite what to expect when she looked out the window in the morning.

It had been a long time since she'd felt this way.

She'd tried to put down roots in Vancouver because her parents had, but look how that had turned out.

Maybe she really was meant to be an eternal nomad.

Only the idea of moving constantly made her a bit uneasy. It brought out all those old feelings. It made her stomach twist.

She was confused and didn't know what she wanted.

Lacey could usually keep control of her emotions—it was how she'd avoided getting attached to things as a child—but she could see already she was getting attached to Thatcher. He stirred so many feelings inside her, to the point that she didn't know what she was feeling at all. She had no control.

It scared and thrilled her in equal measure.

As she finished clicking through the pictures, a notification popped up. Though she tried to ignore it, it was large—magnified almost—and ran right across the screen. There was no way for her to avoid it. It was to Thatcher, it was from the Duke of Weymouth and the first line that was previewed read, Dear Son…

CHAPTER SIX

LACEY LEANED OVER the side of the railing on the flat-bottom boat as it made its way slowly up the inlet, but instead of focusing on the beauty around her, all she could think about was that email notification.

She couldn't believe Thatcher was the missing heir. He was going to be the next Duke of Weymouth. Sorry… Edward. Thatcher wasn't even his real name!

Obviously he was in hiding, but why?

When she saw that notification pop up, everything had started to click into place. Eton, Cambridge, his attitude whenever she said he seemed familiar and his attitude about the British aristocracy.

Every time she mentioned those things, he tensed right up, and now she understood all too well why. What she couldn't understand was why he was hiding away.

Why are you *hiding away, Lacey?*

She ignored that thought.

She glanced up at the trees, craning her neck to see the canopy, but she couldn't—as they say—see the forest for the trees. All she could see was Thatcher. And the fact that she didn't know anything about who he really was.

Who are you, *Lacey?*

She didn't know that either.

It bothered her that Thatcher had lied about who he was.

What else was he hiding?

Lacey sighed. Why did she always fall for the wrong man?

The thought made her spine stiffen. She was not falling for Thatcher. She was here to work, not rush into another romance. Not that she would now consider her relationship with Will a great romance…

Her stomach knotted, and she shook her head to clear out all the conflicting thoughts running around in circles in her mind. She should be focusing on the beauty around her. Not on Thatcher and his secrets.

"Enjoying the scenery?"

Lacey glanced over her shoulder, groaning inwardly and trying not to openly show her disdain when she saw it was Matt Bain, the first officer of the *Alaskan Princess*, standing next to her.

He thought he was charming, and maybe he was to the right type of woman, but that wasn't her, and she was annoyed that he was intruding on her thoughts. She'd rather obsess about Thatcher and all the feelings he was stirring up inside her than chat with Matt.

"I am," she said politely. "It's nice and quiet."

She was hoping that Matt would take the hint, but she was dismayed to see that wasn't going to be the case.

"It kind of gets boring after multiple trips. It all blends together, you know?"

"The trips or the trees?" she asked.

"The trips."

She nodded. "You've been doing this for a while, then, I assume?"

"Yes. Waiting to get my own command. Hopefully somewhere warmer." He grinned at her, a grin that was clearly supposed to charm her and make her simper, but didn't. And what was with everyone sharing all the plans they had for their futures with her? It was the last thing she needed when she couldn't get her own life together.

The future was blank to her. At least when she would move around as a kid, she had her parents with her for support.

"That sounds like a good plan." She turned to look back at the trees, hoping that he would leave. She just wanted to be alone with her thoughts.

"You know, if this trip goes smoothly, I'll be able to choose my own crew, and I'll need medical staff."

"I think Dr. Bell has other plans."

"I don't mean him," Matt said with a hint of derision in his voice. "I mean you."

"I'm a newbie here."

"So?" He grinned again and moved a bit closer to her. "I was so impressed with how you handled the situation when that man fell from the balcony."

Lacey really didn't know how to respond to that, so she avoided looking at him and focused on the bow of the barge. It was then that she saw one of the other passengers start to shake. The woman's knees seemed to buckle, but even though she righted herself, it was a red flag to Lacey, and the warning bells began to go off.

She moved away from Matt and walked toward the woman, and as she began to wobble a bit more, Lacey quickened her pace.

"Ma'am?" Lacey called out. Only she was too late. The woman started to fall, and all Lacey could do at that point was try to cushion her landing.

Thatcher was waiting at the boat launch on the *Alaskan Princess*. He'd gotten word over the radio that one of the barges had to turn back because of a medical emergency. He'd been about to get on another barge to meet the other boat halfway, but then he'd learned that Lacey had been there, and the passenger was stable.

It relieved him to know Lacey had it in hand, but he felt bad that she was going to miss out on the grizzly bears.

If the situation was reversed, you'd have done the same.

Patients first.

Always.

Sort of like how your father put the estate and his title first?

Thatcher ignored that thought. It was different. He was saving lives, and if he was in the position his father had been in, with a wife and children, he'd make time for them.

And he would certainly never cheat on his wife, the way his father had constantly cheated on his mother.

The barge docked, and he climbed aboard to find Lacey had the patient lying down. At least the patient was conscious, even if her color still didn't look good.

"What happened?" Thatcher asked, setting down his medical kit next to them.

Lacey didn't look at him. "Ms. Lawrence here fainted and took a while to come to."

Thatcher cocked an eyebrow. "Her blood pressure?"

"I couldn't take an accurate reading, but it was low and sluggish. It seems to be coming back stronger now."

Thatcher pulled out his blood pressure cuff. "Well, we'll see what it is now."

"This is Dr. Bell, the ship's doctor, and he's going to run some checks on you," Lacey said calmly.

Ms. Lawrence nodded.

"Hello, I'm Dr. Bell. Can you tell me how you're feeling?"

"Better," Ms. Lawrence said shakily.

"Ms. Lawrence said she's a diabetic," Lacey stated.

"I think I didn't have enough to eat this morning," Ms. Lawrence said. "I was so nervous about the bears and being on a smaller boat."

Thatcher smiled at Ms. Lawrence. "That's understandable."

He glanced up at Lacey to find she was staring at him intently. Usually it would cause a physical reaction in him. He liked when their gazes would meet, but this was different.

She was acting odd.

Like she didn't know him. As if he was a stranger to her.

Like she saw him in a new light.

His stomach twisted in worry, and for one fleeting second, he thought she might know who he really was…but that wasn't possible.

Still, there was a pit in his stomach. It gave him pause.

When she left the infirmary to join the shore excursion, something had changed.

He hoped he was wrong and that she didn't know who he was, because that would change everything.

You don't know that.

Except, he sort of did. Everyone who knew he had a title coming to him treated him differently. They weren't genuine.

And when he walked away from it all, all those people who had claimed to care for him turned their backs. It saddened him to think of Lacey being just like everyone else. It made him anxious.

Focus on the patient.

He didn't have time to worry about Lacey and why she was acting so weird, and he wasn't here to make friends. He took this job five years ago to finance his dream.

To be independent.

Not contemplate a romance.

That was the furthest thing from his mind.

Is it?

"Your blood pressure is better, Ms. Lawrence,

but still a little lower than I'd like. You should probably head back to your cabin for now. Nurse Greenwood will accompany you and then come to check on you a bit later, once you've had some food and a rest."

Ms. Lawrence nodded and continued to sip the orange juice one of the crew members had handed her when she and Lacey had docked.

Thatcher packed up his equipment, and Lacey asked him to step away with her for a moment.

"You okay?" he asked stiffly, trying not to worry about her behavior.

"Fine," Lacey said, but she didn't sound fine. He noticed how her eyes darted away, and she wouldn't look at him squarely.

"You don't seem fine."

"How should I be?"

"I would assume annoyed you had to come back," he said.

She smiled, but it was forced. "There is that, but it's my job."

Thatcher smiled back at her, trying to ease the tension. "Well, I'm sorry."

"Don't be. I can always come another time."

"On the next cruise?"

"I haven't decided on that. Although Matt Bain was on the barge and offered me a job on his ship next year."

Thatcher cocked an eyebrow. "His ship?"

"He has big plans too."

He snorted. "I'm sure. Well, good for him."

"To be honest, I'm not sure if I'm going on another cruise or not."

"Can you take care of Ms. Lawrence and report back to me?" he asked.

"Of course." She still refused to look him in the eye.

He stared at her, confused as to what could have come over her.

It's not your concern.

And it wasn't.

When this cruise was all said and done, he'd finally have everything he'd ever wanted. He could disappear into the Yukon and no one would ever know where or who he was.

He'd be happy.

Finally.

Will you?

Lacey took a deep breath and left Ms. Lawrence's cabin to walk back to the infirmary. She wanted to tell Thatcher about that notification she'd seen, and ask him about it. He had been lying to her.

Maybe he wasn't even really a doctor…

She couldn't finish that thought without laughing at herself for even contemplating it.

Of course he is. He knows what he's doing.

At least, that's what she was telling herself. He talked about schooling and a practice on Harley Street, which was where all the posh physicians in London were. She was being silly. Yet he had lied to her about who he was...

She couldn't help but wonder why.

Thatcher was going to be the next Duke of Weymouth. Why hide that? She couldn't exactly recall the reasons the papers had suggested why the heir had up and left, and a large part of her was hoping he could—and would—explain it.

It's not your business.

He didn't know everything about her. Why should she know about this?

She knew that was true, but she also knew she couldn't work with someone she didn't know or trust. She'd been lied to so many times before— heck, she'd almost married a liar!—and yet here she was, completely attracted to one.

He didn't exactly lie. He just didn't tell you about his past.

Either way, they were still strangers.

Still, she wanted him to know she saw the no-tification. She didn't want to hide that from him, and she hadn't done anything wrong.

Lacey took another deep breath and stared at the closed door of the infirmary. Her anxiety was running away with her. She had to remain calm and focused.

Just ask him and admit you saw it.

If he got mad, he got mad. It wasn't as if she actually read the email…though she did search him on the internet and saw the photos, and it was a bit surreal to know she was working with the missing future duke.

She opened the door and walked into the infirmary.

Thatcher was sitting in his office and glanced up from his desk.

"How is Ms. Lawrence?" he asked.

"Good. She tested her blood sugar and it was low, so she's going to rest, and I'll check on her later."

"I'm sorry you missed the excursion."

"I'm here to work. It's fine." She bit her lip and shut the door to his office behind her.

He frowned. "Is everything okay?"

"I don't like to deceive anyone." Her voice was shaking, and she was sweating.

His brows furrowed. "Neither do I."

"When I was looking at your photos earlier, an email notification popped up on the screen. I didn't click on it, but I saw it. I'm sorry."

His eyes widened. "A notification?"

"Yes." Her heart was pounding and thundering in her ears, and her palms were sweaty.

Thatcher folded his hands on his desk. "Thank you for being forthright about it."

"You're welcome. I don't believe in deception, and I have to trust the person I work with, so I wanted you to know I'm not nosy by nature."

"I appreciate that."

She could hear the edge in his voice, and she knew he was questioning what she might have seen. She'd be doing the same thing if she was in his position, wondering which email he saw and whether she had something she needed to hide.

"I know who you are, Thatcher. Or rather, Edward. And who your father is."

His lips pressed together in a thin line, his eyes sparking. She knew his back was up and she was treading on dangerous ground.

Thatcher didn't respond right away. He just tented his fingers and stared at her.

"Do you?" he finally asked, a bit stiffly.

"You're the missing heir. You'll be the next Duke of Weymouth." Her heart felt like it was in her throat.

She'd seen something personal, something secret about him, and she felt nervous knowing that because she wasn't sure about how she would feel if the situation was reversed. Not that she had any secrets to hide. She was just a private person.

She had never really let anyone in that deeply before.

Not that she was anywhere as interesting as a missing heir.

She just needed him to know that she'd seen the email and she wouldn't betray his trust because it wasn't her business. His secret was safe.

Her conscience would be clear.

Thatcher said nothing. His eyes narrowed. "How much?"

Lacey shook her head, not understanding what he was saying. "How much of the email did I see? I told you, just the notification—who it was from and the first line of the body of the email, which included the word *Son.*"

"That is not what I meant," he snapped, standing up and leaning over the desk, staring her down in a way that unnerved her and shook her to her very core. "How. Much?"

"I don't understand," she said back just as fiercely.

Lacey didn't know what he wanted. Did he not believe her that she only saw the notification? Was he insinuating she'd read the actual email? Because she hadn't.

"I mean how much money do you want from me to keep this quiet?"

CHAPTER SEVEN

THATCHER HAD FELT sick to his stomach when Lacey said she saw one of his email notifications. He hoped it was something else she saw, but of course it wasn't. It was the one email he didn't want her—or anyone—to see.

The one from his father. And his father used his actual given name.

Edward.

Which he hated. It was the same name as his father's.

He preferred his middle name of Thatcher. Which his mother gave him. Still, Lacey saw it. There was no denying it, and it made him feel numb.

And now he had to pay her off. Why else would she tell him she knew who he was?

It was blackmail.

Only she seemed quite confused that he was asking her to name her price.

"Why would I want money?" she asked. "Are

you insinuating that I'm trying to blackmail you?"

"Isn't that what you're doing?" he asked.

"No. And frankly, I'm insulted you would think that."

"You're insulted?" he asked, surprised.

She crossed her arms and frowned at him. "I am, rather."

"Why did you tell me, then, if you don't want money?" It was now his turn to be confused.

"I felt bad I had seen the notification, and I don't like deception. My ex-fiancé lied to me, cheated on me, so I don't like liars, and I didn't want to pretend I hadn't seen it. I wanted you to know that I knew and that your secret is safe with me. I wouldn't betray your trust."

Thatcher was growing increasingly confused, and he sat back down. He wasn't used to this.

The concept of feeling safe with someone was foreign to him.

The only person he felt safe with had been his late mother. His mother had never lied to him or hurt him, like his father had. She had been his home, and then she'd died, and he'd tried to be that for Michael. Only he couldn't.

Usually people wanted something from him, and he had assumed the same of Lacey. He thought she wanted money.

You don't know her. You can't trust her.

Which was true. He didn't know her, and he didn't feel safe that she had this knowledge about him. For five years he'd been in hiding, and now someone knew who he really was. It was bad enough that Michael had finally tracked him down to guilt him into coming home.

Now Lacey knew who he was.

But she didn't want his money. She said his secret was safe with her. Thatcher wanted to believe her, but couldn't.

"I'd rather just pay you off," he grumbled.

Lacey smiled. "Jeez, you are a jaded one."

He couldn't help but chuckle at that. "It's what I'm used to. So is this why you were acting so weird when you came back on the barge with Ms. Lawrence?"

Lacey's cheeks tinged pink. "Yes. It was weighing heavy on me, knowing something you obviously didn't want the rest of the world to know."

"Okay. Well, thank you for telling me. I was a bit worried about your behavior."

"I'm sorry for that, but I felt it was right you knew that I knew who you were, Your— What do I call you?"

"Thatcher or Dr. Bell, please. Nothing needs to change, and I don't really enjoy the proper titles."

"Do you also not enjoy being called Edward?" she asked.

"No. I hate that name. It's my father's name. Thatcher is my middle name and my preferred moniker."

Lacey sat down across from him. There was a slight smile on her luscious lips. "So, you're really a physician?"

"Of course I am. I wouldn't have been in this job long if I was faking it."

"I know. I was just joshing. Not many dukes are doctors. None that I'm aware of anyway."

"Well, I am. I do need money to live."

"Your father is wealthy…" she said. "You don't necessarily need to work."

"And that's just it. My father is wealthy. I am not. I needed a job. I didn't want to rely on my father. That was never my style. I wanted to earn my keep. Always."

"Is your brother a doctor too?" she asked.

"No, he manages the estate…and our father. He does the work I technically should be doing as heir. The problem is, I was never really into it. I would've probably been really bad at it if I had given it a go."

"That's all I need to know."

"What? That I'd be a bad land manager? Or that you thought I was a spoiled rich kid pretending to be something I wasn't? This isn't some kind of dramatic novel."

"I know. I'm sorry I asked, and I'm sorry I saw the email notification. I really won't say anything. I promise." She crossed her heart to emphasize her point. "And I don't want your money. That's not why I told you."

He wanted to believe her, but he was having a hard time doing that.

He didn't know her. How could he trust her? He couldn't trust anyone...

His father had made him promises of being more available after his mother passed away, but he wasn't.

Kathleen swore she loved him, but she didn't. She loved the title. The money.

He wanted to believe Lacey, he truly did, but how could he?

The reality was that he was at her mercy, and he'd have to put his faith in her promise. He'd have to trust this complete stranger with a secret that he'd kept to himself for a long time.

"Thank you," he said, breaking the silence. "I appreciate it."

Lacey stood. "Well, I'm going to check on Ms. Lawrence again, and then I'll be back. I'm sure there will be some minor injuries as the barges full of passengers return from kayaking."

"You can almost always count on it." He stood as she moved to leave. "Lacey?"

She turned and looked back. "Yes, Dr. Bell?"

"Would you like to have dinner with me tonight? In my quarters, away from the others, so I can properly thank you and we can talk more about this?"

She smiled, a big, beautiful one that reached her twinkling eyes. His pulse was racing, and he felt like an awkward teen again in that first flush of youth, instead of the jaded, crotchety man he knew he'd become over the years. She was a breath of fresh air, and she made him want to breathe more.

"I'd like that very much," she said.

"Great. Around seven?"

"Sounds good. I'll see you in a bit. We'll meet at the boat launch when the passengers come back and assess the damage from kayaking."

He smiled and chuckled softly. "Okay. Perfect."

She shut his office door, and he sank back down in his chair.

What had he just done?

He hadn't been out on a date with someone since Kathleen.

It's not a date. It's a thank-you-for-not-blabbing dinner.

It had been five years since he'd admitted to

anyone who he actually was. Even to himself, if he was honest. He'd put it all out of his mind when he'd left and just focused on his work and his dreams. It was scary having that knowledge—his truth—out there, but a bit freeing too.

He could be himself with Lacey and not have to worry about tripping up.

It almost meant trouble.

He was already fighting a strong attraction to her, and he didn't want this to mess up his tenuous hold on his control. He didn't want to fall for her. He didn't know what she wanted for her life. He didn't know where her heart lay. She'd just gotten out of a relationship and was even still wearing her engagement ring. He doubted she was ready for anything.

This was his last cruise.

He couldn't wait for her.

He had plans.

Nothing was going to stop him from his future and buying his land.

Nothing was going to keep him away from his dream.

Lacey didn't know why she'd agreed to come to his quarters for this private dinner. She should've politely said no, only she couldn't.

Thatcher obviously wanted to talk, and they hadn't had much of a chance when the passengers returned from the shore excursion because, as she had suspected, there were a lot of cuts and scrapes, and a sprain or two.

Thinking about having dinner with him alone later made the butterflies in her stomach do backflips. She was so nervous, and she'd never been this nervous about having dinner with a colleague before.

What was it about Thatcher that made her feel this way?

Excited.

Anxious.

A jumble of emotions.

Why was she letting herself be so affected by him? It wasn't like her to get emotionally attached or invested in people—she was too used to always getting hurt in the end. Every time they left a place when she was a kid, her heart had broken. She was used to being up-rooted, but it still hurt to lose all the friends she'd made, knowing they likely wouldn't keep in touch. Only Carol had stayed in her life, but friendships were always different—harder—when they were at a distance.

It's why she locked away all of her emotions and allowed her work to keep her busy through the years.

She knew Thatcher would hurt her in the long run, just like all the others, but she couldn't help but accept his dinner invitation. He wanted to talk to her, to let her in, and she wanted to let him in too.

Her pulse raced as she thought about him, wondering if he might put his arms around her again.

She had to stop thinking about him like that.

Lacey wasn't sure what her future held, and Thatcher had plans practically etched in stone.

Plans that didn't include her.

And he could still go back to the UK and take up his dukedom, or whatever it was called.

The point was that Thatcher had options, and she didn't even know where the heck she was going once the ship docked back in Vancouver. Lacey had to get control over her runaway thoughts and this crazy anxiety that was gripping her. This was just dinner between two colleagues, nothing more. And she needed to keep reminding herself of that.

Still, her hand shook as she knocked on the door of his quarters.

He answered and smiled when he saw her. "Welcome."

He opened the door wider and ushered her in. His quarters were larger than hers, and he had a small enclosed balcony.

"Wow, I guess it pays to be a senior officer."

"You're a senior officer too," he quipped.

"Yes, but my cabin is nothing like this. Of course, I'm new and you've been the ship's doctor for a while, so that probably has something to do with it."

"True."

"Or maybe you're just lucky," she teased.

"I am, I suppose. I also took a slight cut in pay to get a better room, and I never take time off, so the captain assigned me this cabin." He motioned for her to come out onto the enclosed glass balcony.

It was only seven, and as it was late August, it wasn't near dark yet. There was a beautiful glow of a higher-latitude sun on the waters of the inside passage that played well with the green of the forests clinging to the land edging the calm waters.

It was beautiful.

She'd been in Vancouver for five years, but she'd never left it, never traveled north like this to see the landscape beyond the city borders.

Work took priority, and because she'd spent so long traveling around as a child, it had felt good to plant roots when her parents had retired there. She'd settled in, met Will and thought she'd have a stable life. Obviously, it wasn't meant to be. It was weird to be uprooted once again now, but on the flip side, she was being reminded of how much she loved traveling. She hadn't realized she was missing it. Even though she'd hated moving around so much as a kid, constantly feeling as though they were leaving almost as soon as they arrived, there was also another small part of her that had always liked seeing new sights, new landscapes.

She missed the adventure.

She missed the north. Alaska, or at least what she'd seen of it so far, was beautiful. The landscape made her think of Yellowknife, reminded her of that excitement she'd felt when her parents drove along that lonely stretch of highway to a city in the middle of the wilderness.

She missed it.

Vancouver, she didn't miss.

Maybe her father was right, and the world really was hers to make what she wanted of it.

"If you're lucky, we might see a pod of orcas go by," Thatcher remarked, interrupting her thoughts.

"Really? I've never seen them in person."

"Aren't you from Vancouver?"

"No, I was born in Toronto. I've been in Vancouver the last five years, but work takes precedence over sightseeing. I know you can go to an aquarium or sea life park to see them, but frankly I don't want to. I don't like captive whales." She sighed and gazed out over the water. "This is where they belong. Wild and free."

Thatcher smiled, his eyes twinkling. "I absolutely agree."

A blush warmed her cheeks, and she found she was suddenly nervous again.

Get a grip, Lacey.

Thatcher pulled out a chair, and she sat down, laughing nervously. "No one has ever pulled out a chair for me before."

"What? Not even your ex-fiancé?" he asked.

"Nope. We didn't go out together much. We were both too devoted to work to make time for fancy dinner dates."

"Well, us Brits are taught manners," he teased. "Well, some of us."

"Ha ha."

"Would you like a glass of wine?"

"Please."

"I've got rosé, if that's acceptable?"

"Very," she replied.

He brought out the bottle from the chiller, uncorked it and poured her a glass.

"Dinner will be here soon. I mentioned to the captain we were having a staff meeting, but I suspect the first officer doesn't quite believe my intentions are honorable."

Her heart skipped a beat as she took a sip of her drink. "Are they?"

"Perhaps," he teased, pouring himself a glass.

Lacey laughed nervously. "I don't know why I'm here."

"I just wanted to thank you for not blackmailing me."

"I would never do that."

"Also, I wanted to mention that we make port at Skagway tomorrow, and since all the passengers are disembarking, we both can enjoy shore leave."

"Great! I'm looking forward to shore leave and Skagway."

Thatcher cocked an eyebrow. "You're looking forward to Skagway?"

"Yes! It's the gateway to the Yukon and the gold rush."

"Are you going to ride the train?"

"No. Probably not. I wouldn't do it alone."

"Why not?" Thatcher asked.

She shrugged. "I don't know. I haven't ever really played tourist by myself before."

"It might be fun."

"It's more fun with friends, I think, and since I don't have any friends on this cruise, I'll sit it out."

"I'm your friend."

Her heart skipped a beat. "What?"

"I'm your friend." He smiled, his gray eyes sparkling. "Or at least, I could be."

Warmth spread through her body. Tears stung

her eyes. She would like Thatcher to be her friend. She wasn't in a place to expect—or accept—more from him, but she could be his friend.

"I'd like that."

"Good. And as your friend, I'll go with you," he offered.

"Really?"

He shrugged. "Why not?"

Before she could respond to his question, there was a knock at the door.

"That must be dinner." He got up to answer the door, and one of the porters wheeled in a cart with their food. She watched him speaking with the porter, stunned and pleased at the thought of being Thatcher's friend.

And nothing more.

Even if there was a part of her that wanted more.

"Thanks, James," Thatcher said, giving the young man a tip.

James smiled. "Just leave it outside when you're done and I'll come by later and get it, Dr. Bell."

The porter left, and Thatcher handed her a covered plate from the room service cart. Whatever was under the cover smelled heavenly—like butter, garlic and cream. All the stuff that was bad for you…and yet tasted so good.

"I think it's shrimp scampi tonight," he said.

"Yum!" She lifted the cover, and after the puff of escaping steam evaporated, she could see that it was indeed shrimp scampi. Her stomach rumbled in appreciation. It was one of her favorite dishes.

"So what were we talking about?" Thatcher asked, sitting down.

"The Yukon and Skagway."

"Right." He smiled. "Not the most riveting of conversations."

She laughed. "I suppose not, but really it was my bad segue into asking you why you decided to settle in the Yukon."

"Because I love it. When I was younger, my father took me on a trip to tour northern Canada, and I was instantly hooked. It was a place I'd always wanted to go, and it surpassed my expectations. You know how you said that the orcas are wild and free? That's how I felt the first time I saw the Yukon."

"You knew right away?"

"I did. I always was fascinated by the north. I read everything I could about it. I was obsessed."

"Why?"

"Why not?" he asked.

"Well, you just come from a completely different world. It's not something I would've expected of a duke."

"Well, I'm not a typical duke. I'm not a duke at all," he teased.

Her heart fluttered again. His smile was so warm, it was dazzling, and his eyes were twinkling again. It made her insides flutter when he smiled at her like that.

It made her weak in the knees.

"No, I suppose you're not," she said softly.

Thatcher laughed. "I think part of what fascinated me about it was influenced by the fact that when my mother was ill, there was this young doctor who was so kind to her. He was from the Yukon, and he'd tell me stories. Impressionable youth and all that, I became obsessed and I read all I could."

"That sounds great. I've never felt such an attachment. I have to admit I'm a bit envious of that. Of course, how could I get attached when I was always on the move?"

Now who's lying?

She loved the north.

The only place that had ever really felt like home had been Yellowknife.

Now she was free. She could go back.

And that thought scared her.

Her freedom scared her.

"You said you liked the north," he prompted her.

"You're right. Some of my happiest memories

are from the short time my father was stationed in the Northwest Territories and Yukon. I have to be honest, though. I try not to think about it. It hurts too much." Her voice shook, and she hated being so vulnerable in front of him. She usually always kept tight control of her emotions.

"Have you ever thought about going back?" he asked gently.

"Every day."

It was a shock to admit it out loud. She was over thirty, and she didn't have anything or anyone holding her back from doing what she wanted, going where she wanted.

And it scared her, the uncertainty of her future. She wasn't really sure she could ever go back.

"You should consider going back if Vancouver doesn't hold your heart any longer."

"I guess I could, but…"

"What?" he asked, the softness of his voice causing her heart to flutter.

"I don't know," she said nervously, fidgeting. "Everyone I knew in Yellowknife is probably gone or doesn't remember me anymore. My friend Carol was the only person from that time that I kept in touch with, and she passed away a year ago from cancer."

It wasn't really home anymore.

Nowhere was.

"I'm sorry for the loss of your friend."

Lacey tried to shrug indifferently, but she was fighting back the urge to cry. Tears were stinging her eyes, and she hated that she was being so vulnerable in front of him.

Tears were a sign of weakness in her mind. A weakness for her, anyway.

And then he reached across the table and touched her hand. The brush of his fingers against her knuckles sent a shiver of anticipation through her.

She should pull her hand away, only she couldn't. Thatcher offered comfort, and she took it. She wanted it.

She craved it.

And then his fingers touched her engagement ring. That brought reality crashing back. She pulled her hand away.

"Thanks. You're a good friend."

"And a good friend rides the train with his friend."

"You don't have to."

"Nonsense, we're taking the train tomorrow. It's been decided," Thatcher said.

"Will we be able to see your land from the train?" she teased, glad for the change in subject.

"No. I don't know where in the Yukon I'll be settling. Somewhere will sing to me, I'm sure."

"And eventually you'll head back to England?"

"No," he said firmly. And in that moment, everything about his countenance changed. The spark in his eyes was gone. His back straightened. It was definitely a touchy subject.

"Not even when you eventually become the duke?"

"No." He was quiet, and he took a sip of his wine. She knew this line of questioning was bothering him. Thatcher was the missing heir, so there were obviously issues he wasn't comfortable discussing. But could one just walk away from a title?

She didn't know.

All she knew was she wanted to change the subject, to steer the conversation back to something light and easy.

"So, after dinner, if there are no patients, do you want to go down to that eighties bar?"

"What?" he asked, almost choking on his wine. "Why?"

"I hear it's good."

"I don't dance."

"Don't all rich men who come from money know how to dance?"

"That's a stereotype," he said firmly, but the twinkle was back in his eyes.

"That's a shame. Although I could show you, if you'd like." She smiled slyly.

Thatcher shook his head. "I don't think that's wise."

"Why not?"

"I'm not the most graceful."

"Oh, come on. You're poised. You're strong. I'm sure you can hold your own on the dance floor."

Thatcher cocked an eyebrow. "I assure you, I have no grace when it comes to dancing."

"Look, you've got me going on a train to the Yukon tomorrow, so the least you could do is indulge me for a dance or two."

"So you *are* going to blackmail me after all," he teased.

"Maybe, in this."

Thatcher poured her another glass of wine and rolled his eyes, smiling. "Okay, I guess I have no choice."

"No. You don't," she teased.

"I have managed to keep from going there the last five years. You're breaking my streak."

"Good. It seems like you could use some fun."

She could also use some fun. She couldn't remember the last time she'd gone dancing.

It had been a long, long, long time.

"Hardly," he groused.

"Oh, come on," she teased. "It'll be fun."

"I'm a hermit. I keep a low profile."

"You'll have plenty of time in the Yukon to be a hermit. We're going dancing." She was a bit nervous, but she was excited. She just wanted to move to the music and not think about anything.

He was frowning, but she could tell it was just an act. He might complain, but he would go with her.

It was fun being with Thatcher. He was willing to give it a shot, but Will would've gotten angry and made her feel bad for asking. Not in a million years would Will have ever gone dancing with her.

She really didn't know what she was thinking being with Will. It was becoming clearer every day that she'd made the right decision coming here.

Lacey laughed, and they finished their dinner chatting and teasing each other about nothing in particular.

It was so easy to talk to him, and she couldn't remember the last time she enjoyed herself more. It was refreshing.

The thumping beats of eighties music filled the hallway on the main deck that led toward the nightclub, Spin Me Round. At least Lacey didn't insist they dress up in neon or crimp their hair.

Not that you could crimp his short, wiry, ginger hair.

He really didn't want to go into the club. There was a reason he was avoiding it. A lot of the crew frequented the bar, and a lot of passengers tended to go a bit overboard. Especially in regard to neon and acid-wash jeans.

It was over-the-top, loud, clichéd, and so not his scene, but Lacey was excited, and he couldn't resist her. He was lonely. He hadn't realized how lonely he'd been until he started spending time with Lacey and felt how fun it was to be with her.

She was easy to talk to.

When she came to his door for dinner, his breath had been taken away when he saw her.

Her hair was down, and she was wearing a soft gray sweater that bared one creamy shoulder. Everything about her look was soft, and it was all he could do not to hold her in his arms.

When he'd reached out to take her small, delicate hand over dinner, he hadn't been thinking straight. It was just meant to be an offer of comfort, and he'd thought she'd pull away right away. She hadn't, and it had felt right to hold her hand in his. But then he'd accidentally touched her engagement ring. That was when she had disengaged, and he realized he had pushed it too far.

He had to resist his attraction to her.

Why? the other part of his brain asked. The part that was attracted to Lacey.

The part that wanted to kiss her.

Lacey knew who he truly was. What if she was acting this way because of who his family was? He hated that those thoughts crept into his mind, but he'd been burned that way before and knew he needed to be careful.

Get a grip.

"The music sounds great!" she shouted as they waited outside the club to get in. She was bouncing up and down, and he hadn't ever seen her so animated or excited.

She was adorable.

And even though he didn't want to be here, he was glad he was here with her.

"How can you tell? It's all so loud."

Although he wouldn't admit it, the music was indeed catchy. The atmosphere reminded him of when he was in college and he and his friends would go clubbing.

It was in a themed club like this that he'd first met Kathleen, and maybe that was why he felt some trepidation—a bit of his lived trauma encroaching on the present. When he went to that club all those years ago, he'd felt out of place and awkward, and then Kathleen had approached him from across the dance floor. She was a beautiful woman, and she'd swept him off his feet, but he'd been younger then and not so hardened.

Thatcher hesitated when the line moved, not wanting to go in, and Lacey reached and slipped her hand into his, catching him off guard. This time it was she who was reaching out to comfort him. She pulled him into the club, the touch causing his blood to heat. Her hand was so tiny in his, and it felt right to hold her. It was reassuring. He knew he should take his hand back once they were inside, only he couldn't.

It was nice holding her hand as they walked into the club and made their way to the dance floor. Then all he could do was watch, mesmerized, as she began to dance. He couldn't even hear the music. All he saw was her as she moved to a popular song. All he wanted to do was stand there and stare at her.

He wished he could be as free as she was. She didn't seem to have any inhibitions. There were no protocols she had to follow. No one was watching her like the world watched him. And he was envious of her freedom. He knew what was waiting for him if he went back to his father's world, or if someone found him. Everything would change. What was he talking about? Everything had already changed when she saw that notification.

After she'd told him what she'd seen and left

him alone in his office, he had opened the email from his father.

It was the first time he had written to Thatcher since he'd left the UK five years ago, following the worst argument they'd ever had. It was just after Kathleen had broken up with him, when he'd gone to see his father. Instead of finding solace for the betrayal, for the broken heart he was feeling, Thatcher was given a cold rebuff and a lecture about duty. That had been the breaking point.

That was when he'd realized he'd never please his father.

That was when he'd decided to leave.

"It's simple. You find another woman to be your duchess," his father had stated.

"Kathleen would've happily been my duchess."

"Then what's the problem?" his father had asked, confused.

"I don't want to be the duke," Thatcher had snapped.

His father's face had gone red. *"What do you mean, you don't want to be the duke? It's not a choice. It's a duty one is born into."*

"And it's one I don't want, which is why Kathleen left."

"You have no choice, Edward. Just like I didn't."

"You have two sons. Let Michael have it," Thatcher had said.

His father's eyes had narrowed. "No. It's your duty. You will be the next Duke of Weymouth. That's how it's always been done. Find a new duchess if Kathleen isn't willing to come back."

"Kathleen doesn't love me."

"What does love have to do with anything?"

That question had enraged Thatcher. His mother had loved his father, but it was obvious his father had never truly cared for her.

Thatcher wanted a woman to love him for him.

Even though his father insisted he had no choice in the matter, Thatcher wouldn't settle for a life he didn't want or a loveless marriage.

He had been unsurprised to find that the email didn't say anything new or different. His father hadn't changed.

For five long years, they hadn't communicated, and yet the old man was still going on about Thatcher's duty and his birthright, begging him to come home and do what was right.

His father couldn't understand that what Thatcher was doing *was* right for him. Distracted by his thoughts, Thatcher made his way off the dance floor to grab a drink.

"She is a firecracker!"

Thatcher spun around to see a couple of guys

talking appreciatively about Lacey. They were right. She did have a spark and did ignite his blood. From the short time he'd known Lacey, he knew she was confident in her work, and that she was strong and tough, but there was a part of her that she kept hidden and controlled.

Almost like a firework getting ready to explode.

He smiled, finished his drink and headed out onto the dance floor as a ballad started, one of those old heavy metal ones, the lead singer screeching about romance over heavy guitar riffs. It was kind of piercing, but he didn't care. He just wanted her in his arms, and he was feeling brave.

"Can I have this dance?" he asked, bowing slightly at the waist.

"Of course." Her eyes were twinkling as she wrapped her arms around his neck and pulled him close, but she trembled slightly in his arms. His pulse was racing, and it was like he was dancing with a ball of flame that sent a zing through his body.

Making him feel alive again.

He felt every nerve ending in his body.

"See, dancing's not so hard," Lacey whispered in his ear.

He chuckled, pleased. "We'll see."

"Be nice."

"No. I think not." He grinned at her, holding her tight against him. His pulse was thundering between his ears, and he could feel her tremble again in his arms as the music slowed.

No one else was there, or at least no one that he noticed.

It was just the two of them.

It was as though time was standing still, and it took every ounce of his strength not to reach down, touch her face and pull her in for a kiss.

He noticed a pink blush had tinged her cheeks. He loved when she blushed like that. She was so stunningly beautiful. He was enchanted by her.

She smiled as she looked up at him, her fingers tickling the nape of his neck. "Would you like some air?"

"You mean leave? Yes. I would like that."

He wasn't a fan of crowded dance floors, and he wanted her alone.

More than anything.

This time he was the one who took her hand as they walked out of the club, and he led her up a set of stairs to the upper deck that was open. They walked hand in hand as the sun finished slipping down below the horizon and the first stars began to creep out.

Lacey stared up at the sky. "It's so beautiful."

He had to agree, but it wasn't the stars that

he was looking at. He didn't care about the night sky.

"Have you ever seen the northern lights?" he asked.

"Yes, but not for some time. I hope we'll see some once we're further north."

"I hope so too." He thought about how magical it would be to kiss her under the aurora borealis.

She was so beautiful, and as they stood there, stargazing, he reached out and touched her cheek. A pink blush crept up her neck, and he felt goose bumps break out over her soft skin. She bit her bottom lip, her big eyes looking up at him through thick lashes.

He couldn't resist. He pulled her into his arms and softly tasted her lips.

His hands went into her hair as she pressed closer, the kiss deepening as he drank her taste in.

What're you doing?

She pushed him away gently.

"I'm sorry," she said breathlessly.

"No. I'm sorry."

He didn't want to rush her into anything. Especially because anything between them would only ever be temporary. He had plans, and she wasn't part of them. He was getting swept up in something. They barely knew each other—she was a stranger. He knew he shouldn't trust her, but he was lonely. Until Lacey came on board, he hadn't realized how isolated he had been in his self-imposed exile.

"I can't, Thatcher. I only just left a man at the altar. I can't... I can't do this."

Lacey dashed away, and he cursed himself under his breath.

He knew she was vulnerable. What had he been thinking, kissing her like that?

Her lips, his body answered back.

Thatcher shook that thought out of his mind. Lacey was off-limits no matter how much he wanted her.

CHAPTER EIGHT

LACEY TOSSED AND turned all night. The feel of Thatcher's lips was still etched on hers, and she touched them in the dark, yearning for more.

She was also kicking herself for leaving.

For one moment she'd almost been swept away. When he took her in his arms and kissed her, her body had melted.

It was like she'd been woken up, like everything that came before had been in black-and-white and suddenly her world was Technicolor.

For a moment she forgot about Will, her wedding…everything.

When it all came rushing back, she'd felt guilty for allowing herself to get caught up in the moment with Thatcher. Like she had betrayed Will or something.

Will cheated on you, though.

And that was true, but she couldn't shake the feeling that *she* had done something wrong.

Will always accused her of being too work-centered and not affectionate enough. She should've seen that as a warning sign, and the more she thought about it, their last fight before she'd caught him cheating on her should've told her what was going to happen next...

"You never pay attention to me," Will had said.

Lacey had looked up from her computer. "What?"

Will had frowned. "Exactly. You work more than me, and I'm a surgeon."

She'd smiled. "I'm sorry. I thought we'd agreed that work came first. You work a lot too, and I just got in the habit of doing the same."

"Well, you barely pay attention to me. You rarely show affection in public," he'd groused.

"Where is this coming from, Will? Why now? You never liked it before."

Will had shaken his head. "I don't know. I mean, our situation together is ideal. I guess this must be a midlife crisis."

"You're not at midlife yet. You're a successful surgeon with a fiancée. Hardly midlife meltdown material."

"That's not funny, Lacey. I have so much more to accomplish," he'd said firmly, but there had been something about the tone of his voice that had made her a bit worried.

"Is it that you're not sure where I fit into all this?" Lacey had asked quietly.

He'd nodded. *"Do you fit into the life I planned for myself? I'm not so sure."*

Will had walked away, and she'd gone back to work.

If she was honest, Lacey hadn't been sure either. Will had laid out his life for himself, and they were only getting married because it seemed like the logical thing to do. They liked each other, but now, looking back, she wasn't sure she'd ever really been in love with him.

Thatcher's kiss had been amazing and rocked her to her very core, in a way Will's kisses never had.

She didn't know what she wanted. This cruise was supposed to be a chance for her to clear her head. Instead, it confused her all the more.

She didn't know what she wanted.

Except to continue that kiss. That kiss that had fired her senses.

It was right to break things off before they got too heated, though. She wanted to be friends with Thatcher, but nothing more. She couldn't commit to anyone when she didn't know what she wanted.

Are you sure? a tiny voice asked in her head, but she shook that annoying little voice away and got up an hour earlier than she had to. She got dressed and ready for her day in Skagway, even though she wasn't sure she even wanted to go after what had happened. If Thatcher wanted to put off their plan to take the train over the White Pass, then she'd be fine with that.

She didn't want to make him uncomfortable.

They could be friends, right?

She just wanted things to go back to the way they were, before that kiss.

Lacey liked working with Thatcher, and she wanted the rest of this cruise and the trip back to Vancouver to go as smoothly as possible.

After she finished getting ready for the day, she headed out of her quarters and made her way to the infirmary, where she and Thatcher were going to meet. The ship was still and quiet as it had docked in the Skagway port overnight.

Soon the rest of the passengers would be getting up and making their way off the ship to enjoy a long day in Skagway.

To distract herself from the silence, Lacey went over the cruise itinerary in her mind. She knew that after today, the ship would depart in the middle of the night on the way to the next port of call, which was Juneau, to view the glaciers, and then out into the Gulf of Alaska to make its way up to Anchorage, stopping along the coast. After Anchorage, the passengers would depart and fly home after three weeks at sea.

Lacey was grateful for the long break from real life. She needed to get her mind straight.

She needed to think.

She took a deep breath and headed into the infirmary.

Thatcher was working on something, but was casually dressed for his shore leave in jeans and a nice sweater. The deep forest green color suited him, and her heart skipped a beat. He turned when she walked in, and she could feel the awkward tension between them.

"Hi," he said.

"Hey," she responded, wringing her hands. "Look, about last night…"

"I'm sorry for bolting."

He smiled, looking relieved. "I'm sorry too. I didn't mean to kiss you."

"I think I was kissing you back," she said, laughing nervously.

"Yes."

Lacey laughed again, softly this time. "Look, I just want things to go back to the way they were. I would hate to ruin our professional relationship, and I would hate to ruin a possible friendship."

He nodded. "Agreed. I wasn't sure that you would come today. I bought two tickets for the darn train, and thought I might have to ride it alone."

"You bought two tickets?" she asked. "I can buy my own ticket."

"I expect you to," he teased. "I'm kidding. It's my treat. I got tickets for the first trip. That way, we can get it done first thing and have the rest of the day open. It's actually supposed to be sunny instead of rainy, which is kind of amazing."

Lacey chuckled. "Well, that sounds great. I'm glad we can put this thing behind us and move on."

Thatcher smiled. "Me too. Shall we go? We can disembark with the rest of the passengers."

"That sounds great."

Thatcher grabbed his raincoat. "Do you have a beanie?"

"No. It's August. Should I?" she asked, confused.

"It can get cold on the pass. We'll hit one of the outfitter stores on the walk to the train and get you some warmer outerwear. Besides, they won't let you back into Canada without the right supplies when going over the White Pass." He locked the infirmary, and they headed to the lower deck, where everyone was disembarking into the port.

"What?" she asked.

"Haven't you studied anything about the gold

rush era? You needed a certain amount of supplies to head to the Klondike or they'd turn you away. I thought you knew that. You were excited to come to Skagway."

"I know it was the gateway, but I'm sorry that I don't remember the exact list of things that prospectors were required to have to go over the pass."

"They needed to take a ton of supplies to survive the Canadian winters in the Yukon, and if they didn't have the right amount of items at the checkpoint, the Mounties would send them back. Sam Steele and all that. You're the daughter of an RCMP officer and you don't know that? For shame," he teased.

Lacey rolled her eyes. "Sorry. I do remember that it was almost like a human chain, just a constant mass of men going over the pass, and that both horses and men would often fall to their deaths."

"So you pick up on the deaths, but not on the supplies. I have to say, Lacey, that's kind of morbid."

They both laughed, and she thought about how good it felt to laugh with him.

It also felt good to feel that tension from their kiss the night before melting away.

They joined the mass of people funneling out of the ship and down a gangway to the dock.

Once they were off the boat, people began to disperse.

Lacey stared around in wonder at the small bay that was surrounded by not only mountains but also other behemoth cruise ships filling the harbor and towering over the small town.

The main part of town was filled with brightly colored buildings meant to attract tourists, but Lacey closed her eyes and tried to picture what it would have been like when this town was founded on the spoils of the gold rush.

The beach would have been filled with cargo that was brought in off the barges and steamboats. There would have been tents, mud and hope for the gold that could be found over the treacherous White Pass. There would also have been absolute despair from those who had lost everything and now needed to find a way to get back home.

That's if they survived, because until the narrow-gauge train was built, the walk was often gruesome, littered with those who had dropped dead of starvation or disease.

Maybe Thatcher was right, and she was a bit morbid.

They made their way past many tour company booths offering passengers cheap tours for the surrounding area. There were wildlife tours, fishing expeditions, dog mushing, helicopter rides to the glacier and more.

As they followed the general direction of the crowd, they passed one of the first stores in the historic frontier town, which sold everything from T-shirts to diamonds to outerwear. Lacey bought herself a pair of woolen mittens and a beanie, and then they walked over to a bakery.

The shop smelled like coffee, sugar and golden sizzling fat. It made her stomach rumble.

"Two coffees and a fry bread, please," Thatcher ordered.

The woman behind the counter nodded and walked away.

"Just one?" Lacey asked.

"They're huge and full of sugar. One is enough, believe me."

When the woman came back, Lacey's eyes widened. It *was* huge. Thatcher took the coffees and Lacey paid, then picked up the freshly made fry bread. It was warm in her hand, and despite the paper wrapped around it, the powdered sugar was everywhere.

They made their way over to a small table, where Thatcher set down the coffees.

"Go on," he said.

"What?" she asked.

"Take a bite." His eyes were twinkling. "It's your first time. Ladies first and all that."

She took a bite, and a whoosh of powdered sugar puffed out as she bit into the warm, heavenly dough.

She couldn't help but laugh.

"How bad is it?" she asked, grabbing a napkin to wipe.

He was chuckling. "You look like you've stuck your face in a snowbank."

"You knew it would do that!" she accused him, laughing.

"Maybe. This is the only shop that does them like this." Then he reached out and brushed sugar from her nose. The simple act made her pulse race and her breath catch in her throat.

He paused and moved away as if realizing what he'd done.

She blushed and handed him the fry bread. "Well, that was an experience."

"It's good, though, right?"

"It is. It reminds me of a beignet a bit."

He smiled, but there was an awkward tension that settled between them again. She hated that.

"Come on," he said. "We better go or we'll miss the train."

After boarding, they found seats near the back.

"You have the window seat, since this is your first time and all," Thatcher offered.

"Why, thank you." She slid into the seat, and Thatcher sat next to her. She set down her coffee cup in the small cup holder. "How long is this trip, anyway?"

"Are you in a rush?" he teased.

"I do want to visit the Gold Rush Cemetery."

He wrinkled his nose and made a face. "You really are morbid."

She laughed. "I just want to see where Soapy Smith is buried."

"Soapy who?" he asked.

"Okay, now who doesn't know their frontier history?"

"I guess between the two of us, we'll have enough information to be know-it-alls on this trip."

"That sounds like fun. So, are you going to answer my original question?"

"Which was what?"

"How long is the trip?"

"Two hours, almost three round-trip. Of course, we could've said bugger it all to the whole day and taken the eight-hour trip to Lake Bennett and back."

"Ooh, that sounds fun, but probably way more pricey."

"It is, and you need slightly more time than we have."

Lacey settled against the seat as the last of the passengers from the various cruise lines boarded the train, and they waited for the final preparations to be made to start their journey over the winding White Pass to the summit.

Thatcher was absolutely exhausted. After their kiss last night, he couldn't think about anything else. All he did was toss and turn, dreaming about that kiss and what it was like to have her in his arms.

It had felt right in a way it had never felt with Kathleen. Then again, he'd thought what he had with Kathleen had felt right at the time, but he'd been proven wrong in the end.

He barely knew Lacey.

Why did he want to continue whatever this was developing between them? The only reason he could think of was the fact that Lacey actually listened to him. She didn't think his plans were crazy like Kathleen had. She didn't try to convince him to go back and take up his birthright.

It may also have been his loneliness that caused him to act the way he did. He'd been irrational, foolish and swept up in the moment.

She was easy to talk to, and it had felt right, so he'd kissed her. And then she pushed him away. She'd been hurt and vulnerable, and maybe he shouldn't have done that.

He was worried he'd scared her off and hadn't been one hundred percent sure that Lacey was going to show up today. So when she walked into the infirmary, he'd been so relieved.

He'd also been relieved that she wanted to continue their friendship, because that's what he wanted too.

It was nice to have a friend again. He'd worked with many other nurses, but they'd never been interested in forming any kind of friendship, and that didn't bother him in the least. Thatcher wasn't sure what was so different about Lacey, but he wanted to continue to find out. He couldn't stop thinking about her.

And he liked being with her.

For the first time in a long time, he was enjoying himself.

He was glad that they were able to work this out. He was glad there was no awkwardness after his faux pas last night. Not that he thought kissing her was a mistake. He just didn't want to push her away.

The only problem was, the more he was spending time with her, the more he didn't want just a friendship.

He wanted more from her, and he was doing everything in his power not to put his arm around her or hold her hand.

There was a moment in the bakery when he'd forgotten that she wanted to be just friends, and he'd come close to kissing that sugar off her nose. Her lips were sweet, and he wanted to taste them again.

It would have been an incredibly intimate gesture. He'd known he shouldn't do it and had stopped himself just in time.

But he was drawn to her.

It would be hard to say goodbye to her when the cruise was over and they went their separate ways, because that was one thing he wasn't sure about when it came to Lacey.

She didn't know where she was going.

And he did.

He glanced over at her as she rested her chin on her hand, staring out the window as the train slowly climbed up to the White Pass. She was beautiful sitting there, so thoughtful.

"Come on," he said, standing up and holding out his hand.

"What?" she asked, startled.

"You can't experience the climb this way. Let's step outside."

"Outside? Are you crazy?"

"It's safe," he said. "There's a platform between cars. Come on."

Lacey took his hand and hers shook in his, which he found endearing. He led her through the jostling car. They opened the door and stepped out onto the platform that connected the cars. There was a spot for them to stand so she could get a real feel of the way the narrow-gauge train hugged the side of the mountain and see the drop down. They could also see a train that had departed after them slowly starting its ascent.

The trees became thinner as they climbed and clung to the precarious side, and her mouth opened in wonder.

"This is amazing. I can see why they called this Dead Horse Pass."

"You seriously have to stop with the death stuff," he teased.

"Sure, sure," she said.

There was a jostle, and as Lacey cried out, he braced himself behind her, his arms going around her. "You're okay."

"My heart is racing," she said a bit breathlessly.

"It's an old train, but it's safe, I promise. Look at the trestle bridge. You can see the glacier, which means we're getting closer to the pass."

Lacey craned her head to look over the side, and he held on tight, making sure that she didn't fall. He could smell her hair. It felt so right being this close to her.

"Do they let us out to walk around up there?" she asked.

"We don't have passports."

"I bet I can. I'm Canadian." She smiled smugly, teasing him.

"You still don't have your passport. The ship does."

"Right." She frowned. "I'm a Mountie's daughter. I should be allowed. I mean, my great-grandfather was a Mountie up in the Yukon."

"I highly doubt your great-grandfather worked with Sam Steele," he said dryly.

"No, but we had a dog who was named Sam Steele." Her eyes were twinkling with amusement, and he couldn't help but laugh with her.

"I don't think that will count."

They stood quietly as they went over the trestle bridge and stared down at the maw of forest, rock and water so far down. His pulse was thundering in his ears.

"Here comes a tunnel," she announced, and he knew it was the last tunnel they would go through before the White Pass.

Thatcher just stared at her. His heart was racing, and his body felt like it was on fire. He was burning for her.

For the first time in a long time, he wanted someone again, but he was scared to open his heart. He wasn't sure that he could do it, even though he wanted to.

Even though he wanted Lacey. Maybe it was because she knew the truth about who he was, and that was incredibly freeing. The tunnel ended and the summit came into view.

There were flagpoles designating the separation of Canada and the US and a small obelisk in memorial for all those pack animals who had died along the route.

The train slowed to a stop, and they waited to make the proper turnaround and head back down.

"This is the boring part," he murmured.

There were a lot of people around him taking pictures, which made him uneasy, and she frowned as she looked up at him, as if reading his thoughts.

"Shall we go back to our seats? There seems to be a crush of people out here all of a sudden."

"I would like that." It was unnerving being in a crowd sometimes. He was always worried that someone would recognize him, and then the press would find him.

They were headed back to their seats when the door from the back of their car was flung open by an out-of-breath conductor.

"Is there a doctor on board?"

Thatcher raised his hand. "I'm a doctor. Is everything okay?"

The conductor was trying to catch his breath and shook his head. "There's a woman in the back car who has gone into labor!"

CHAPTER NINE

Lacey didn't have time to ask why a woman who was nine months pregnant was allowed on a train that climbed to this elevation—she could ask that later. Right now she had to jump into action. As soon as the conductor had announced that a woman was in labor, she took off like a shot, with Thatcher close at her heels.

"I'm a midwife," she said.

"Thank God," the conductor said, still breathless. "Can you follow me?"

"Lead the way, by all means," Thatcher urged.

They followed the conductor, who had clearly checked the other cars for a doctor, as the passengers they went by were abuzz, and all eyes were on them.

She had noticed how uneasy Thatcher had been when there were a bunch of people snapping pictures of the White Pass around them, so she could only imagine how he was feeling now, with all the other passengers staring at them.

The last car was used for the staff, so no other passengers were present, and it was apparent that the woman and her partner had made their way back there for privacy.

"I found a doctor and a midwife," the conductor announced, the relief in his voice palpable.

The woman in labor was panting and in pain, on the floor with a blanket covering her. Lacey grabbed the first aid kit that had been brought out and pulled on a pair of gloves.

"I'm Lacey Greenwood. I'm a nurse practitioner and certified midwife. This is Dr. Bell."

The woman in labor nodded, and her partner smiled shakily. "I'm Sherry, and this is my wife, Robyn. This is our first!"

Lacey smiled encouragingly. "Congratulations."

"What do you need?" Thatcher asked Lacey.

"Water and emergency blankets, for starters. I also don't want this train moving until this baby is delivered."

The conductor left to speak to the engineer.

"I'll be your nurse this time," Thatcher offered.

Lacey nodded and examined Robyn. She was fully dilated, and Lacey could make out the top of the head.

"Okay, Robyn, on your next contraction, I need you to push." Lacey placed her hand on the top of Robyn's abdomen and felt the next contraction building up. "Robyn, I need you to bear down now and push for me."

Robyn pushed with all her might, her wife, Sherry, holding her shoulders and encouraging her.

"Good," Lacey told Robyn. "You're doing so well."

The contraction ended, and Lacey could see the baby was moving and getting ready to turn.

"I knew this was a mistake," Robyn whimpered between contractions.

"What was?" Lacey asked.

"Coming on the train," Sherry said. "We thought we had time. She's only thirty-five weeks. This was our last hurrah."

Lacey nodded. "Well, babies do have their own timeline."

"Oh, God," Robyn moaned.

"Here comes another contraction. I need you to push, Robyn. Hard. Come on," Lacey urged.

It only took a couple more pushes, and the baby was born, screaming heartily into the world.

"You have a brand-new Canadian," Lacey teased. "It's a boy."

Sherry and Robyn began to cry with joy as Lacey cleared the baby's throat, and the little boy cried even harder.

Thatcher was smiling as he clamped the cord for her.

"Sherry, would you like to cut the cord?" Lacey asked.

Sherry nodded, crying with happiness as Thatcher handed her the scissors. She cut her son's umbilical cord, and Lacey wrapped the baby up and handed him over to his parents. She couldn't help but smile as the new family got to know each other.

Lacey then delivered the placenta and ensured that all looked good.

The conductor entered the carriage. "Is everything all right?"

Lacey nodded. "You can tell the engineer it's safe to head back down now, and if you can arrange for an ambulance to meet the train at the Skagway station, that would be excellent."

The conductor nodded. "I'll do that straightaway."

Lacey cleaned up with Thatcher's help as the train started with a chug, and the conductor got on the speaker to announce the birth of wee little Christopher and to congratulate the new family.

"You did amazing," Thatcher said to Lacey. "I was so glad you were here to do this. It's been a long time since I delivered a baby. It's certainly not something you usually see on a cruise ship."

Lacey laughed. "No. I suppose not. I never

thought that particular skill of mine would be used on this trip, if I'm honest."

"Well, usually it's not," he said, and then he smiled at her. "Of course, this has been one for the books."

She chuckled. "It has, hasn't it? I'm glad I was able to help."

She looked back at the happy family. It was such a beautiful scene. She always thought she wanted to have children, but then there was a part of her that didn't think she could have them. Maybe it had never been on her mind because she wasn't sure where she was going to end up for so long.

Will hadn't wanted a family anytime soon.

Another sign she had missed. Why did she ever think that Will had been right for her?

She loved babies.

She loved kids, and looking at Sherry and Robyn holding their brand-new baby, there was a part of her that was envious of their love. There was a part of her that longed to have what they had. Her parents had always given her love. They had been her only constant.

Warmth spread through her. A warmth that she hadn't felt before, or at least hadn't felt in a long time. The warmth she'd felt when she and her family had been settled in Yellowknife.

When she had friends and they stayed in one place for a long time.

When it had felt like home.

And then her father got a new posting and she'd had to say goodbye to that home. She'd had to say goodbye to her friends, her teachers, everything she loved about that place. It had broken her heart.

That was when she'd decided never to get too attached to things or people.

It was just easier when you knew you'd eventually have to move on. She hadn't thought about those feelings of connectedness and warmth in a long time, but seeing Robyn and Sherry with their new baby brought it all back. Suddenly it seemed to be the exact thing she wanted.

And for the first time in a long time, she thought about her future and about what she wanted. It made her nervous.

It made her wish for things that she thought were long forgotten.

Things she had thought she'd put aside and buried away, but apparently hadn't. She didn't realize that it was all still simmering, there below the surface.

It was unwelcome.

It was unsettling.

Because she suddenly wanted it so much, and wasn't sure she'd ever get it.

* * *

Lacey watched the ambulance take the new family off to the hospital so that the doctors there could check over the newest member of Sherry and Robyn's family.

"You did a good job on that train," Thatcher said, coming up beside her.

"Thanks. I didn't have to do much other than catch," Lacey joked.

"Were they part of the *Alaskan Princess* cruise?"

"No," Lacey said. "I had the paramedics contact their ship. I didn't know what the protocol was in a case like this, but that seemed to make the most sense."

"I don't know either. I haven't had to deal with something like this before."

They walked away from the station and headed back to town. She was still feeling a bit sad and didn't know what to say.

"Are you quite all right?"

"How do you mean?" Lacey asked.

"You've gone quiet. Something changed up there after the baby was born."

Lacey shrugged. "I don't know. I guess I was thinking about how lucky that little family was."

When Will had told her he didn't think kids would happen soon, she'd sort of just buried that desire for a family deep down. After all, she cared for Will and had been with him for two years. Not having a family right away wasn't a reason to walk away from a marriage, was it?

Except it was. She realized that now. When she saw that little baby with his parents, it had made her feel all warm and sparkly on the inside.

She wanted that.

She always had.

"I thought you had a good childhood?" Thatcher asked.

"I did, but we were always on the move, and that birth just made me think of the time when we stayed put for a while. It made me think about how happy I was. I didn't really realize how much I missed it until I saw them. So it made me a little bit…"

"You were reminiscing?"

"Yes." She smiled. "I was. So, sorry if I'm a bit maudlin."

"I know something that will cheer you up."

"It's okay. I don't really need to visit the Gold Rush Cemetery."

"I know, and that's not what I was suggesting," Thatcher said. "I was thinking we could go to a saloon and grab some lunch. One of those really cheesy places with really bad food. What do you say?"

She laughed. "You want to take me to a place that has bad food?"

"No, good food, but bad for you."

"That sounds great." And it did. She was hungry, and she needed to take her mind off everything. She needed to bury those feelings deep down again.

She wasn't sure what her future held, and she didn't want to think about something she probably wouldn't ever have.

Thatcher knew that something had changed with her. She had two great parents, but she was sad too. They were more similar than he'd thought, because seeing that new happy family had also made him long for a family.

A wife and children.

Only that wasn't in his future, and it made him melancholy. One thing was for certain, Lacey did an amazing job helping that mother deliver her baby.

He was so impressed.

He loved working with her, and it was an amazing moment, watching a new life come into the world. That was something he didn't get to see very often.

There was a point in his past when he'd thought about having children with Kathleen, back when he still believed Kathleen loved him. But after Kathleen left him, she took with her all his dreams about having a family. Now it was something he thought he could never have, so he didn't waste time dwelling on it. Instead he focused on the plans for his land and a small practice.

When that little boy was born, though, it had forced him to think about that lost dream he had.

What they both needed to do was have a bite to eat to cheer them up and celebrate the fact that there was a new baby boy in the world. This was shore leave, and it would be their last until they got to Anchorage.

Then, once they were back in Vancouver, he was done. It saddened him to think that his time with Lacey was finite.

This was his last trip. He'd be heading off to the Yukon to start his life over, and Lacey would be off somewhere else too. That thought gave him pause.

The Rusty Saloon was close to the port where all the cruise ships docked, and it was dressed up to be like one of the old-time frontier saloons. He'd never bothered to eat here, but he had kind of wanted to. He'd heard the food was good, and the few times he'd come into Skagway, he'd peeked inside, but never actually grabbed a table for himself as it was always so busy.

A grin broke across Lacey's face as they walked through the swing doors. The sign said

to seat yourself, so they found a small booth that was tucked away in the corner with a window that faced out over the pier. They could see the ships, the water and the mountains.

"This is a lot of fun," she said excitedly. "Do you come here every time you're in Skagway?"

"No. This is my first time here."

She frowned. "You said the food was good. I assumed that meant you'd been here before."

"I heard that the food was good, but I never came here on my own. So I guess having lunch here is a good way to finish off my last visit to Skagway."

"You might come back to Skagway again."

"Probably not. I plan to hide myself away in the Yukon."

She cocked her head to one side. "Why hide, though?"

"I think that it's pretty obvious. So I'm not found."

"Your father knows where you are."

He tensed when she mentioned him. Thatcher didn't want to talk about his father. Not now. The email hadn't said anything new. He'd heard it all before.

"He knows the general area where I am. It's no secret, though. He's known my whole life where I wanted to go. It's not just him. It's also every-

thing else I want to hide from and ignore. I don't think that you quite understand the embarrassment of your fiancé cheating on you and finding out via the papers. The whole world watching every single moment of your life. Nothing about my life was private."

Her cheeks flushed pink, and he realized it was the first time he'd mentioned that he'd been cheated on.

"I'm sorry that happened to you," she said quietly.

"Look, I didn't mean to get angry with you. It's just…my situation is unique."

"Is it?" she asked. "We were both cheated on."

"Yes. But in my case, she did it because she only ever wanted me for my title," he whispered. "Whereas I wanted her. She wanted the money and the fame, not me, and my choice to not accept my birthright was her breaking point."

She nodded.

He cocked an eyebrow. "What about you?"

"Honestly, now that I think about it, I should have known it was coming, but I honestly didn't see the signs. We were together for so long, and marriage seemed like the right next step."

"Sounds like you were going to settle."

He noticed she was fiddling with that engagement ring again. It annoyed him that someone else had given her a ring first.

He was…jealous.

Lacey sighed. "It was…logical. I'm not sure that I believe in romantic love at this point. I've been hurt too many times."

Thatcher was disappointed with that answer. He wasn't sure why, though, as it really didn't affect him. Except…he did believe in love. He'd been blinded by it and burned by it, but he still believed that romantic love existed for some people.

Definitely not for him, but he thought it was sad that she didn't believe in love, especially when she was such a loving, caring healer.

"I still believe in love. Not that it's for everyone," he said, and he saw a strange expression cross her face. Almost like she was disappointed.

"This is awful," she said.

"What?"

"Us. Two jaded, maudlin creatures sitting here in such a fun place with jobs on a cruise ship, doing what we love, and we're complaining about not having or believing in romantic love. It's kind of a bummer."

He chuckled at that. "Yes, it kinda is. So, then, what do we talk about?"

"Well, did you ever email your dad back?"

"My *dad*?" he asked, teasing. "I would never refer to him as Dad. I've always just called him Father."

"Don't be so pedantic, you pelican." There was a twinkle in her big blue eyes, and it looked like everything that had been bothering her before had melted away.

"That is the first time I've ever been called a pelican as an insult before."

"I couldn't think of anything else." She nodded. "First bird I saw outside, I suppose."

"Is a pelican so bad?" he asked.

"No, except they kind of stink, so maybe." She smiled, laughing slightly.

"Thanks." He sighed. "No, I haven't talked to my father or responded to his email."

"Do you think you should? Maybe he's worried about you."

"He's not worried about me," Thatcher intoned.

"You said he didn't know where you were, but had a general idea. I mean, I know my parents would be worried if they didn't know where I was."

"Remember, our childhoods were completely different."

Which was true. Her parents both loved her, and it seemed as though they made sure she always knew it.

Thatcher understood that his mother had cared for him and Michael, but she died when he was young and Michael was barely more than an infant. As for his father, he was just absent and really had no interest in them until they got older.

Even then, it was all about duty.

It was all about pomp and circumstance.

It was cold and forced.

There was nothing warm or cheery about his childhood. That was why Thatcher had always sworn that if he had children of his own, it would be different.

Except, he wasn't going to have children. It was kind of hard to plan for a family when you didn't plan on having someone to share your life with.

"What're you going to order?" he asked, trying to read the very large menu, but he was unable to focus on any of the words.

"I'm surprised that they have poutine on here," she murmured. "I'm going to have to try it and see what it's like. You don't often see it outside of Canada."

"Probably because Skagway is so close to the Canadian border. It's only a two-hour drive or so to Whitehorse."

"I didn't realize it was that close. Well, I'll definitely have to taste their poutine, then. See if they do it justice."

"That is something I haven't tried," Thatcher admitted. "I've been in Canada for five years, granted mostly doing cruises, but still haven't tried poutine, and I haven't the faintest idea what is in it."

Her mouth hung open. "Are you crazy? Have you been living under a rock?"

"Sort of. I haven't the time or inclination to pay attention to much except working and planning out the next stage of my life in the Yukon."

Lacey shook her head. "I can't believe you don't know."

"Well, what is it?"

"French fries, gravy and cheese curds."

"That's it?" he asked. "That's what the hype is about?"

"Split a large plate with me and you'll see it lives up to said hype."

Thatcher folded his menu. "Fine. Since you're buying."

Lacey smiled and closed her menu too. The waitress then came over, and Lacey ordered the largest plate of poutine they had and a couple of pops. She then chatted with him about how different places in Canada sometimes called it *soda* and sometimes called it *pop*. Since her parents were from Toronto, they called it *pop*, and that's what she grew up saying.

It was so great to talk to her about nothing.

It helped him to forget everything else.

And that was a dangerous thing indeed. Dangerous for his heart, because he couldn't deny any longer that he was falling for her.

Even though he had plans and Lacey didn't fit into any of them.

She could, a little voice said in his head, but he didn't want to get his hopes up.

They finished their lunch, and he had to admit that the poutine hadn't been terrible. It was quite good, actually. Lacey admitted that the poutine was good, but not the best she'd had. Apparently it was fairly passable, especially for a restaurant that was outside Canada.

For the rest of the afternoon, he tried not to let his mind wander to the what-ifs when it came to Lacey Greenwood.

He just wanted to enjoy his day with her.

Their last shore excursion. In Juneau they would have to stay on board the ship because it was such a short trip, and then they would head out into the Gulf of Alaska, following the marine highway to finish off the cruise in Anchorage.

At least in Anchorage they could disembark for a day before they headed back to Vancouver. Though he'd been looking forward to it, it suddenly made him sad to think that his last cruise with the *Alaskan Princess* was coming to an end and that his time with Lacey would soon be over.

Apparently he was a sucker for punishment, falling for a runaway bride.

CHAPTER TEN

THE SHIP HAD left in the middle of the night when it got clearance from the port authorities, but there was a storm as they headed to Juneau from Skagway, and the ship was moving slowly as rain lashed at its sides.

With the rougher weather, some of her original patients were suffering miserably from seasickness again.

Lacey was also feeling a bit miserable, but it wasn't the motion of the ship that was bothering her. The only thing making her sick was the turmoil of her own emotions. She'd had such a brilliant time with Thatcher in Skagway, especially when they had been on the train to the White Pass and he took her out on the little deck that connected the cars so they could stand outside and watch as the train wound its way up the high mountain pass.

It felt like they were on top of the world, and when his arms came around her, she'd felt safe.

Thatcher made her feel safe in a way she hadn't in a long time, and she'd wanted to stay in that moment forever.

She could see clearly now that she had loved Will, but it was different. If it had been the two of them on that train ride, neither would've said much besides polite small talk, and he certainly wouldn't have stepped outside to enjoy that moment. Truth be told, he probably would've been bored by the whole thing, whereas Lacey had found it thrilling.

And the fact that she was there with Thatcher and feeling all these things was even more confusing.

The whole day—from the birth of the wee baby to the pretty good poutine at the saloon—had been an experience that she would never forget. The thing terrifying her, though, was that she didn't want her time with Thatcher to end, even though she knew it was going to end sooner rather than later.

He'd made it clear that this was his last trip.

She needed to figure out what to do with her life. Lacey thought that by now she would have some idea of what she wanted after this cruise ended, but she still wasn't sure. The cruise was fun, but she felt a bit lonely, and she missed the hustle and bustle of the hospital. So to carry on cruising didn't seem like the right fit for her.

She also missed delivering babies, and there wasn't much of a demand for that on a ship.

And the main thing holding her back was the fact that she wasn't sure that she could handle an Alaskan cruise without Thatcher working alongside her. It would just bring up all these memories, and it would hurt.

That thought shocked her.

It would be painful when he left, and that concerned her. She didn't want to feel that kind of pain ever again, and yet every day they drew closer to Anchorage and then the voyage back to Vancouver. Where she would have to say goodbye to him.

Lacey shook all these confusing thoughts from her mind as she finished the last of her checks on the patients and made her way back to the infirmary. She hadn't seen Thatcher since last evening when they'd boarded the *Alaskan Princess* as he'd gotten called away to see a patient and she'd headed to her quarters.

She'd done some paperwork but was still ignoring her personal emails.

She wasn't quite ready to read an explanation from Will or Beth.

When she walked into the infirmary, Thatcher was sitting at his desk, and she could see him working on some charts. He didn't look up when she came in.

"How are things?" he asked, continuing with his paperwork.

"Everyone is okay. I handed out some more anti-nausea meds." She set her case down and began to throw out the used items and put away the medicine she had left over.

"Great," was all Thatcher responded.

Something had changed. It bothered her. Gone was the playful man she had spent the day with in Skagway. Now he was distant, and she didn't know what she had done wrong.

Does it matter? You want to keep your distance too.

It would be easier on her heart. It would make it easier to say goodbye.

Maybe starting the separation now meant she wouldn't feel any pain when their friendship ended. There had always been an expiration date on this relationship—not that it was a relationship—and she had to accept that.

Lacey sat down at her small desk and began to make notes in the charts of the various passengers.

She could hear the rain and the water lashing at the side of the bulkhead. It sent an eerie feeling down her spine. Something was off about this whole day, and she wasn't sure what was going on.

The PA system came on.

"Dr. Bell and Nurse Greenwood, please report to the upper deck. Medical emergency."

Lacey leaped up and grabbed emergency gear off the shelves.

Thatcher came out of his office. "Do you have your raincoat?"

"No, why would I?"

He pursed his lips and tossed her a green slicker. "I have extra."

"Thanks."

They quickly gathered everything they'd possibly need, and she pulled on her raincoat. She was worried about what they were going to find. Why did she think that a cruise would be an easy job and she'd have time to think?

Since she'd arrived on board, it had been go, go, go.

Lacey followed Thatcher through the passages as they made their way to the upper deck and out onto the exposed portion. Even though it was August, the rain was cold, and the wind was blowing hard. The ship was rocking a bit, and the rain was coming in sideways. It stung at her face.

Thatcher's lips were pressed together in a firm line. She could feel the worry coming off him, and she could feel it in the pit of her stomach.

Suddenly she was terrified.

He turned and looked at her. "Are you okay?"

"I'm fine."

He nodded, and they continued on their way to the bow of the ship, where there was a crowd of crewmen gathered.

As the crowd parted for Thatcher, her heart sank to the soles of her feet. She saw it was Harvey, the man who had fallen from the upper deck when they had been leaving Vancouver.

"What happened?" Thatcher asked.

"He fell overboard. His wife said he fainted and went over," someone from the crew said.

Lacey knelt down on the other side of Harvey. There were blankets on him, but he was soaking wet and his lips were blue, as were his fingertips.

It didn't look good.

"He's breathing," Thatcher shouted over the rain. "How long was he in the water?"

"A while," the crewman said. "Thankfully, I was on deck and able to drop a GPS sensor when he fell."

"That is fast thinking. You probably helped save his life, Crewman," Thatcher stated.

Lacey worried her bottom lip as she pulled out more blankets from the emergency kit. Thatcher leaned over Harvey, calling his name, but he wasn't responding. He was breathing, but he was unconscious.

"His left pupil is blown." Thatcher cursed under his breath and looked up at her. They needed to get him to a hospital. There was nothing more that they could do for him here, other than keep him stable.

"How far are we away from Juneau?" she asked with trepidation as she cleaned up one of his bleeding head wounds.

"A while still," Thatcher said. He looked up at the crewman. "Get a backboard, and we'll take him in out of the rain. He needs to get warmed. And call in the coast guard. A helicopter can land on the deck. We need to get this passenger to Juneau ASAP."

"It'll be a rough landing," the crewman said. "This storm is dangerous."

"It doesn't matter," Thatcher shouted. "I need to get this man to Juneau or he'll die."

The crewman nodded and left to call the coast guard.

This storm was more intense than she originally thought.

Thatcher and Lacey worked to get Harvey stabilized, and once they'd secured him to the backboard, they carried him out of the rain, into the interior of the ship. Lacey was able to start an IV she'd gone to get from the infirmary and get some warm fluids into him.

The crewman who had dropped the GPS device came running back. "The helicopter is on the way. The captain has come to an all stop to wait for the helicopter."

Thatcher nodded and then turned back to Harvey.

"Hold on, Harvey," Lacey whispered.

Thatcher glanced at her, and their gazes locked. He gave her a half smile, but it was grim. She knew, just as he knew, a closed head injury and such a long fall into frigid waters were not good. Harvey needed more medical attention than they could offer him right now.

"I'm going to accompany Harvey to Juneau," Thatcher said. "I want to make sure he's taken care of, so I'll need you to man the infirmary until I get back."

"Of course," Lacey said.

Soon they heard the distinct sound of the helicopter's whirring blades over the rain and thrashing sea.

First Officer Matt Bain and a couple other officers had donned rain gear and everyone went to help load Harvey into the helicopter, while another officer tried to calm Harvey's wife, June. She would have to wait until they docked at Juneau to join her husband at the hospital as Thatcher had to be the one that went on the helicopter with Harvey.

The wind was rough, and Lacey had a sinking feeling in her stomach as the boat swayed in the waves. Even with the stabilizers, the storm was still significantly rocking the boat. It was a strange storm. It was all strange, actually, and that sinking feeling she was experiencing was upsetting. One that she had never experienced before. She was worried for Thatcher going on that helicopter in this storm.

It took every ounce of her strength not to reach out and ask him to be careful like she wanted to do.

She had to remind herself that he wasn't her concern, and the only concern was Harvey, but a lump formed in her throat as they loaded Harvey onto the helicopter and as she watched Thatcher board behind him.

He glanced back at her as the door shut, and she was glad for the rain so that he wouldn't see the tears of her fear rolling down her face. There was a storm, and the helicopter could crash.

She ran back to shelter as the helicopter's blades began to whir again and then lifted it off the deck of the *Alaskan Princess*.

"Do you think he'll be okay?" someone asked, coming up behind her.

"I hope so," Lacey whispered to herself, answering the question, but not turning to look back at whoever asked it.

Although it wasn't Harvey that she was thinking about. She was worried about Thatcher, and that surprised her. She was worried about his safety. This storm was like nothing she had ever seen, and as the helicopter rose into the sky, the wind was blowing it around like it was a leaf.

Her heart stood still, and she held her breath, watching it fly away, worried something would happen to him.

It made her heart hurt thinking that he might be in danger. She would be worried until they docked in Juneau and Thatcher came back on board the cruise ship.

Thatcher had been trying to keep his distance from Lacey, trying to keep things professional, but when he saw her as the helicopter lifted off, all he could see was the pain on her face. He could see the worry etched in her eyes. As if she was worried about him. Was that possible?

He was kind of anxious about the ride too.

He didn't particularly like helicopters, but they needed to get Harvey to the Juneau hospital as quickly as possible.

It tore at his heart to not be there with Lacey to tell her that he was going to be okay, but he had to tell himself that she wasn't his concern. They weren't in a relationship. They had only kissed once and shared some fun times together. She'd made it clear she wasn't ready for anything more serious, and he respected that.

Yet no matter how much he tried to remind himself of that or remind himself of the heartache that Kathleen had caused him, he was still drawn to Lacey, and when he saw her standing on the deck in the rain, all he'd wanted to do was protect her. Wanted to reassure her that he'd be fine.

Once they got to Juneau and landed on the roof of the hospital, there was a trauma team waiting to greet him. He was able to go over Harvey's history with the team while the patient was taken down for a CT scan, where internal bleeding was found.

They also found a blockage in one of Harvey's arteries, which was the probable cause of his fainting spells.

Thatcher remained in the waiting area while Harvey was whisked into surgery and the blood was evacuated from his head wound.

When Harvey was stable in the intensive care unit, June arrived and Thatcher explained everything to her, he knew that he could head back to the ship.

The captain was in the waiting room and met Thatcher as he left the intensive care unit.

"How is our patient?" Captain Aldridge asked.

"Stable. The surgery was successful. He's still intubated, but they're taking good care of him. They plan to address the blockage causing all of his fainting issues tomorrow, but they think it will be a straightforward procedure, and he should make a full recovery."

Captain Aldridge smiled. "Good work, Dr. Bell. You handled that well."

"Well, it was lucky for Harvey that there was a crewman close by, and that crewman had the foresight to drop a GPS device into the water."

"I know, and I'm going to promote him. I wish you would stay with us, Bell. You're a good physician."

Thatcher acknowledged the remark with a smile. "I know. It's been an honor serving under you. If you're in the mood to promote people, though, then might I suggest you promote Nurse Greenwood? She's the most exemplary nurse I've ever worked with."

Captain Aldridge nodded. "Noted. Shall we head back to the *Alaskan Princess*?"

Thatcher nodded. "That would be great."

"I would like you and Nurse Greenwood to join me at the captain's table tonight for dinner, and I'll have the crewman who dropped the GPS join us too."

"Thank you, Captain Aldridge."

They walked out of the hospital, where a hired car was waiting to take them back to the ship. He was sure that Lacey was on edge to hear about

Harvey as he'd been at the hospital for several hours now.

Most of the passengers were still out exploring Juneau, and Captain Aldridge told him that the ship would leave port a little bit later than scheduled that night. They would make up the time as the weather was clearing up and the Gulf of Alaska was surprisingly calm. No one would miss their flights in Anchorage.

The captain continued to drone on, but Thatcher only half listened. He was exhausted.

What had felt like a matter of minutes was actually hours, and though he didn't much feel like having dinner at the captain's table tonight, he couldn't say no.

All he wanted to do was take a hot shower and a nap, but he knew that he would have to see Lacey first, let her know what happened with Harvey and tell her about the dinner.

He'd been hoping for such a calm last cruise, but this had been the busiest he'd ever had. Maybe Lacey Greenwood was cursed. He smiled thinking that. She'd only cursed his fragile heart.

He cared about her, and he'd miss her.

He shouldn't have gotten so close. It was clear that Lacey wasn't ready as she was still wearing her ring.

He was so jealous of her ex. He wished he had been the one to give her the ring, because she wouldn't have run away. He wouldn't have given her a reason to.

Just as he thought, Lacey was waiting in the infirmary when he walked in. She looked like she hadn't been to sleep either.

"Thatcher!" She moved to give him a hug but then hesitated, which he was half relieved, half disappointed about. Even though he knew he shouldn't encourage it, he wanted a hug from her.

He could definitely use a hug from her. In his five years of sailing on the *Alaskan Princess*, he had never lost a patient. Harvey had been the closest call he'd ever had.

"Harvey made it through his first surgery," Thatcher said, trying not to yawn too much.

"He did?" Lacey sank back down in her office chair. "What was wrong? Do they know why he was fainting?"

"Small arterial blockage. An EKG wouldn't have picked it up. They're going to clear the blockage tomorrow, but he made it through his surgery today. They evacuated the brain bleed and released the pressure from the head trauma. He was stable in the intensive care unit when I left, and June was with him."

"She was so upset," Lacey said.

"You looked upset too."

"What do you mean?"

"When the helicopter was taking off, you looked worried." There was a part of him that was hoping she was worried about him, because then maybe it meant that she cared about him, but there was another part of him that didn't want to hold out hope for that.

"I was worried about that helicopter in the storm." She turned back to her charts, her expression hidden. "I was glad to hear that you... that you both landed safely in Juneau."

"Were you?" he asked softly.

"Yes." Her smile wobbled as she looked back at him. "The weather was so rough."

"It was. I'm okay," he said gently.

"Well, I'm really glad." When she said that, his heart skipped a beat, and he wished he could take her in his arms again. To reassure her.

"Yes. Well, he should be okay. That's the end of their cruise though, unfortunately," he said, then cleared his throat.

Lacey nodded. "A crummy way to end a vacation, but I'm glad he survived going overboard."

"Same."

"You look exhausted. Would you like some coffee?" she asked, getting up and heading to the coffee machine.

"Thanks." He walked into his office and sat down in his chair, leaning back as his eyes began to droop.

"Why don't you head back to your quarters and have a nap?"

"Later," he murmured. "Tell me what happened while I was gone."

"Nothing," she said.

He cocked an eyebrow. "Nothing?"

She shrugged. "Nothing. Should be a quiet night. Go to bed early."

"I can't." He groaned.

"Why?"

"We've been invited to the captain's private table for dinner tonight. He wants to honor us and the crewman for saving Harvey's life."

"Then you need this." Lacey handed him a cup of coffee. She smiled at him sweetly.

"Thanks." He took a sip, but he really didn't want coffee. What he really wanted was sleep.

"So, dress whites tonight?" she asked.

"For me," he murmured. "If you have a formal dress, you can wear that."

"Okay." She turned to leave. "Well, try to get some rest before dinner tonight."

"I will."

She left the room, and he leaned back, clicking on his computer and seeing another email from his father.

A couple, in fact.

Thatcher scrubbed a hand over his face and shut off his computer.

He didn't have the mental energy to deal with the Duke of Weymouth today.

He didn't have the energy for much, not even for keeping Lacey at bay and protecting his heart.

CHAPTER ELEVEN

BEFORE LACEY LEFT the infirmary, she checked on Thatcher and found him asleep at his desk, his hand wrapped around his coffee mug. She couldn't help but smile, watching him sleep, leaning back in his chair. He looked so peaceful. It made her heart flutter.

The ship had left the port of Juneau and was trying to make up time to get out into the Gulf of Alaska and finish the last leg of the cruise. She had been busy making house calls and came back to check on Thatcher. She didn't want to disturb him, but she had to leave to get ready for dinner in the captain's private dining room, and she was sure he had to get ready too.

She knew it was to thank them for helping save Harvey, but really she would rather not have dinner with the captain, and it looked like Thatcher wasn't in any kind of shape to either. She was just so exhausted. Emotionally and physically spent. She'd rather just go to bed.

Thatcher had been gone almost eight hours after the incident happened, and it had turned her stomach to think about how she felt when that helicopter took off in stormy weather—like her heart was firmly lodged in her throat. She had so many fears the helicopter was going to crash that she couldn't breathe in that moment. And she couldn't remember the last time she'd been that worried.

Those eight hours were long, wondering what had happened to him. She'd tried to work, and she'd tried to concentrate on other stuff as the ship made its way to Juneau, but she couldn't stop thinking about Thatcher. She'd kept wondering what was happening and wished she could've been there to help him. It would've put her anxiety at rest, to know he was safe.

It had driven her crazy, which freaked her out. Lacey prided herself on having better control of her emotions. What was it about him that changed her perspective? Why was she letting herself get so attached to him? Especially when she still couldn't even really process what had happened with Will.

In her past relationships, when things ended, she moved on. The same with Will. She caught him in the act with Beth, and it was just like all those other times.

It hurt, but she left.

The idea of leaving Thatcher, on the other hand, physically hurt.

And the only thing she could compare it to was that time when they had to move away from Yellowknife, and she had to say goodbye to her friends, her teachers and the home she loved. When they went to the next posting, she'd moped. She was depressed, and then she saw how it was hurting her parents to see her like that, so she sucked it all in. She learned how to deal, so it wouldn't hurt so much.

Then she met Thatcher, and everything she had learned to deal with—all of her carefully constructed walls—came crashing down. Suddenly she was dealing with a bunch of emotions she didn't know how to deal with.

All she knew was she was falling hard for Thatcher.

Lacey had to get control of these emotions before the end of the cruise. If she was going to move on with her life, she had to learn to be on her own, because she didn't know where her life was heading.

She moved into his office as quietly as she could and gently took the coffee mug from him so that he wouldn't spill it all over his computer.

Thatcher woke with a start. "What time is it?"

"Five. I was going to leave and get ready for dinner now."

Thatcher blinked a couple of times. "Right. Yes. Do that. I should get ready too."

"I was just going to dump your cold coffee. I thought it would be better if I dealt with this rather than have you spill it everywhere."

"Thanks. Well, at least I got a power nap in before tonight." He moaned and scrubbed a hand over his face. "I hate these formal dinners. I hated them when my father would hold them, but usually those were complete black tie affairs and involved members of the royal family. If you think a captain's dinner is bad, then try one with royal protocol. It's exhausting."

"I can imagine. I think I'll pass on that," Lacey said. "I would not do well with rules and protocol. I would definitely say the wrong thing or do the wrong thing and end up in the Tower."

Thatcher laughed. "Go get ready, and I'll see you at the captain's private dining room. I'll be more alert then, I promise."

"Okay."

She left his office, dumped the cold coffee and washed the mug, and put it away. She cleaned up the rest of her stuff and then headed to her quarters.

Whatever tension had been between them when they boarded after Skagway was gone. It felt like it had before and she was relieved.

She just wanted this last half of the trip to go smoothly.

It didn't take too long for her to get to her cabin, and thankfully she had a nice black dress that she had packed for the honeymoon. It was nothing spectacular, but at least it would work for tonight. She took off her scrubs and shoved them in the ship's laundry bag, then headed to the shower. A nice hot shower would help her clear her head.

Her phone rang, surprising her because the last couple of days she hadn't been able to get cell service.

She picked up her phone and saw it was a call from her dad.

"Hey, Dad!" she answered, trying to sound happy, even though she wasn't.

"Lacey! I wasn't sure I would be able to get a hold of you. I kept getting the message that the user wasn't in an area with service."

"Well, that's true. We've been at sea and in some remote spots."

"That sounds like fun!"

"Yeah." It had been fun, but she just couldn't muster real enthusiasm, and her father noticed.

"What's wrong?"

"Nothing. Just tired. It's been a lot busier than I expected it to be. Including a delivery."

"You delivered a baby on the cruise ship?"

Lacey laughed. "No, in Skagway. Not one of our passengers. I was on the train with...a friend."

She didn't know why she didn't just tell him about Thatcher. It wouldn't be strange—Thatcher was her colleague—but she felt guilty.

"Well, it sounds like you're busy enough. I would ask you to tell me about all the interesting cases, but I know you can't because of patient confidentiality and all of that. I just wanted to check in on you. Will said you haven't been responding to his emails."

"I haven't had time to respond to his emails," she said, annoyed. And it surprised her that she was so annoyed.

For the first time since the incident on what was supposed to be her wedding day, she was pissed.

"I know. I'll tell him."

"I'll get to them when I can. I have to go soon, Dad. Dinner is at set times."

"Okay. Be safe, and I'll see you in a couple of weeks."

"Bye, Dad." Lacey ended the call and swallowed past the lump in her throat.

She wasn't sure what was happening to her, but she had to get control over this. She didn't have time to feel these things. What she needed was to focus on her next step and what she wanted after this cruise was over.

You want Thatcher. You just can't have him.

She shook that thought away, mad at herself for thinking about something so foolish...even if it was the truth. She glanced down at her hand again. She was still wearing the ring. It annoyed her.

She didn't want this attachment anymore.

She was done.

Lacey pulled the engagement ring off, set it on the counter and took a deep breath to calm her jangled nerves.

Thatcher was feeling a bit more alert, but not completely recovered. He was still exhausted and was uncomfortable in his white dress uniform.

There were a couple other people who were in the dining room, including the crewman Derek, who had been there when Harvey fell and threw the GPS tracker into the water. Derek looked excited to be here, and Thatcher couldn't blame him.

Derek deserved the accolades, but Thatcher just wanted this dinner over and done with so he could go to bed.

The door opened to the private dining room, and he glanced over his shoulder and saw Lacey walk in. She was absolutely stunning. The only other dress he'd seen her in was her wedding dress, and the way she looked now took his breath away. Suddenly he was very much awake.

She had looked beautiful as a bride, but this little strapless black dress she was wearing was gorgeous. It hugged her curves and left nothing to the imagination. His gaze roved over her hungrily, and his pulse kicked up a notch. His blood heated as he let his gaze linger over her long legs, her hips and her breasts.

Her honey-blond hair wasn't pulled back. Instead it hung down in silky waves over her shoulders.

The only thing on her neck was a simple string of pearls.

There was a pink blush to her cheeks, and when she met his gaze, that pink blush deepened. His heart beat just a little bit faster then.

Lacey walked over to him. "Am I dressed okay?" There was a nervous edge to her voice.

"Why would you ask that?"

"Because there are several people staring at me."

"It's not because you're inappropriately dressed, which you're not. It's because you look amazing."

She dropped her head, and her blush deepened. She tucked a strand of hair behind her ear.

"I didn't have a formal dress. Just this old black velvet thing that I love."

"It suits you." He hoped his voice didn't shake. He couldn't take his eyes off her. "Would you like a drink?"

"I would love one. I'm so nervous, and I have no idea why."

Thatcher smiled, and they walked over to the small bar.

"How can I help you?" the barkeep asked.

"A white wine would be great."

"How about prosecco?" the barkeep suggested.

"That sounds great too," she said.

The barkeep turned to him. "And you, Dr. Bell? What would you like?"

"Whiskey. Neat, please. Thank you."

The barkeep turned to prepare their drinks.

"All this fuss," she murmured. "Just for doing our job."

"I know, but Derek, the crewman, is eating this up. He doesn't know it, but he has a promotion headed his way, and he deserves it. He thought quickly and probably is more responsible for saving Harvey's life than we were. In stormy seas, with how long it can take for a cruise ship this big to stop and turn around to rescue someone…well, it could easily become impossible to find someone in time."

"I never really thought about that."

"No one does. It was actually my first 'man overboard' situation in the five years since I started working on the *Alaskan Princess*. Since you arrived, things have been a bit busier."

Lacey laughed nervously. "I don't think that's a good sign."

"It's fine. It just makes work more interesting."

The barkeep handed them their drinks, and they walked away from the bar as the captain's private waiter made his rounds with hors d'oeuvres.

"So now we're at sea for a week?" she asked.

"Yes. We'll be passing some beautiful sights, though, like Kodiak Island, and we'll be heading out to the Aleutian Islands and be close to the Bering Sea. Really the westerly edge of the Americas."

"That's really neat. Don't those islands have volcanoes?"

"Yes, but we're not in any danger."

They were making small talk, but he couldn't think of anything else to say to her, other than repeatedly telling her how beautiful she was, because that was all he could think about. How absolutely stunning she looked in that dress.

How much he wanted her.

He hated that feeling. He hated the way he

burned for her, the way she filled his thoughts, but he couldn't help himself, and he didn't know why he was fighting it at this point.

"This is incredibly stuffy and boring," she whispered.

He chuckled. "Agreed."

Captain Aldridge walked over to them.

"The other two people I wanted to thank personally," Captain Aldridge said.

Lacey smiled brightly at the captain. "Thank you for inviting me, Captain Aldridge."

Captain Aldridge nodded. "Well, of course. You two have been on the go this voyage, and your work has been absolutely exemplary. I have to tell you again, Thatcher, I'm really sorry to see you go."

"I'm sorry to leave too, Captain. I have enjoyed working with you, but it's time to move on," Thatcher said.

"Where are you off to, old man?" another crewman asked.

Thatcher really wasn't interested in talking to anyone. He just wanted to be alone with Lacey. "The Yukon. I'm going to buy some land and open a small practice."

"That sounds…uh…great." The other crewman turned and left the conversation as Lacey tried not to laugh.

"That sounds wonderful. I'm envious, Dr. Bell," Captain Aldridge said.

"I'm looking forward to it," Thatcher said.

"Well, enjoy your evening." Captain Aldridge excused himself to go greet other guests.

"Maybe you'll change your mind and join the first officer's new ship," Lacey teased.

Thatcher rolled his eyes. "No thanks. Besides, he didn't get the Caribbean but a maritime East Coast cruise."

Lacey chuckled behind her hand, and Thatcher couldn't help but snicker a bit.

"Well, so much for his hope of seeing all the ladies in string bikinis," Lacey teased.

"Did he really say that?" he asked in disgust.

"He did. He wanted to 'enjoy the sights.'"

"Especially you." The words slipped out, and he couldn't believe he'd said them.

Pink tinged her cheeks. "What?"

"Oh, come on. You don't think he would appreciate seeing you in a skimpy bikini? I know I would." His blood froze.

Thatcher had been thinking it, but he didn't mean to actually say it out loud.

Though Lacey didn't look offended. She crossed her arms and cocked one of her finely arched brows. "Really?"

"I'm so sorry."

"No, you're not," she teased.

"I didn't mean to say that."

"I don't mind when you say that," she told him.

His heart skipped a beat, and he just stared at her. She was smiling so sweetly, and she was so close he could smell the honey scent of her shampoo. He recalled how soft her lips were and how good it felt to have her in his arms.

"Lacey," he whispered.

"Dr. Bell!"

He groaned inwardly and spun around to see one of the other officers burst into the dining room, looking around frantically until he found them.

"What's wrong?" Thatcher asked.

"There was an accident while break dancing, and it appears someone actually did break something."

Thatcher groaned inwardly and set down his whiskey.

Lacey sighed, and she set down her drink too.

"We're coming," Thatcher said.

He was glad for the distraction, but not for another accident.

This cruise seemed to be cursed. Like the ship of the damned.

The passenger was groaning in the middle of the floor of the nightclub. The lights were on, and the other passengers had been removed. Thatcher had everything he needed on board to set a broken bone, and he hoped that it was just something simple, or they would have to arrange for another helicopter to come to the ship.

At least this wasn't a life-and-death situation.

Lacey kicked off her heels and knelt down on the floor.

"What happened?" Thatcher asked the few people who were remaining.

"Raymond was showing us some moves he used to do as a teenager, and when it came to the twist on his head, he screamed, and there was a crack," a woman said. "I'm his wife, Loretta."

Thatcher winced. "Well, let's have a look, Raymond."

Raymond nodded, and Thatcher cut off his Relax shirt. The moment that he did, he could see the bump on Raymond's clavicle.

"I think you've broken your clavicle, Raymond. We have to get you to our X-ray." Thatcher motioned and had some staff help him with a backboard.

He and Lacey worked to get Raymond onto the backboard and strapped down.

"Loretta, you can come with us to the infirmary," Lacey said over her shoulder.

Loretta nodded.

Thatcher had to get an X-ray done before he

even thought about trying to set anything. He was hoping it was a simple fracture that he could just immobilize and treat with painkillers. Anything worse and they would have to get Raymond off the ship and to a hospital for surgery.

Back in the infirmary, Lacey got the X-ray machine ready, and they put on the draping they needed to protect themselves and Raymond.

It was apparent that Lacey had done this before, because she knew how to drape the patient properly to get films. His last nurse didn't. In fact, if he had that same nurse still on this cruise with all the injuries and what happened with Harvey, Thatcher probably would've gone bonkers. Lacey had obviously worked in trauma and the operating room. She knew how to do so much more than his last nurse, who had worked in a simple clinic before the cruise.

Lacey was more like his right hand. She was a partner.

"Okay, Raymond, I need you to stay still so I can get some clear pictures."

"Okay, Dr. Bell."

Lacey placed the last piece of protective draping and then came behind the screen with Thatcher as he took the X-ray.

The picture came up on the computer instantly. It was definitely a clavicle fracture, but it looked like a hairline fracture and probably wouldn't require surgery. He breathed a sigh of relief when he saw it.

"Well, at least we don't have to call the coast guard to come and get him," Thatcher said. "We'll have to immobilize his arm with a sling and give him a script for painkillers, and when we get to Anchorage in a week, he can get it rechecked."

"We'll just have to keep an eye on him this week at sea. No more break dancing," Lacey said, smiling.

"Not for Raymond, anyways. Do you want to break the news to him?"

Lacey frowned. "That's a terrible pun."

"Yeah, I realized the moment I said it that it sounded bad."

"I'll let him know that his break dancing days aboard this ship are over."

"I'll get a sling."

Lacey nodded and went to deal with the patient while Thatcher grabbed a sling. He was going to have to cut the rest of Raymond's shirt—which was probably one of the original relics from the eighties—off, but it had to be done so he could adjust Raymond's arm.

When he reached the exam room, Lacey had already removed Raymond's shirt, and Loretta was with them. Raymond was clearly starting to feel the effects of the morphine and was relaxing.

"I'll give him some more painkillers, but after a couple of days, he'll just need acetaminophen for the pain. I would avoid ibuprofen," Thatcher said.

Loretta nodded. "Should we get this checked out before we board our flight back to New York in a week?"

"I would," Thatcher said. "It looks like a hairline fracture, but it's such a long flight, it wouldn't hurt to get it checked out. I'll give you my discharge notes and a copy of the X-ray for the doctors in Anchorage."

Loretta smiled. "Thank you, Doctor. He's forty-eight, and I told him he doesn't have to relive his glory days, but he wouldn't listen."

"Relax," Raymond slurred. "Reach out and touch me."

"Those are not the lyrics. Not at all," Thatcher replied dryly. "Sit back and relax, Raymond."

Loretta rolled her eyes, and Lacey chuckled under her breath.

"Sorry I had to ruin your shirt, Raymond," Lacey said. "You can have it sewn back together."

"I would've burned it," Thatcher said.

Loretta and Lacey were laughing, and Raymond just lay there as Thatcher put the X-rays up on the light box and manipulated the arm so it was immobilized against this chest. Then he showed Loretta how to arrange the sling and explained that it needed to be kept tight.

By the time the sling was on, Raymond was dozing on the exam room table.

"I'll get a wheelchair," Lacey offered. "And then I'll push him back to your quarters."

"No, I can do that," Thatcher said. He didn't want Lacey ruining her dress, and he knew he would be able to handle Raymond a bit better. The man wasn't big, but he was tall.

Lacey brought out a wheelchair, and Loretta woke Raymond enough to get in. Thatcher helped them get back to their quarters and settled Raymond into his bed, leaving Loretta with the medication she'd need and his pager number in case Raymond spiked a fever or anything else happened.

He steered the wheelchair back to the infirmary, where Lacey was waiting to clean it with sanitizing wipes.

The rest of the clinic had been cleaned, which was a welcome sight. And then he realized that Lacey was barefoot.

"Where are your shoes?" he asked, confused.

"I kicked them off in the club. One of the waitresses there picked them up for me and left them outside my quarters. I can't kneel down properly in heels. I'm good, but I'm not that good."

"Sorry you didn't get a dinner with the captain in his private dining room. I'm sure he'll make it up to you."

She made a face. "No, that's quite all right. Like I said, it was a bit too stuffy for me. I'm someone who likes simple things like poutine and fry bread."

Me too.

And he loved Lacey for it all the more. She was a breath of fresh air. She wasn't demanding. She didn't ask for anything.

So different from Kathleen.

Still, their lives were going in different directions, and he couldn't give up his dreams, the things he'd been working on for the last five years, for the chance of a romance with Lacey. Especially as Lacey had made it clear when they kissed that it was a one-time thing.

She didn't want a relationship. Not that he could blame her—she had just gotten out of a relationship—but if she wanted him, he would take her with him to the Yukon in a heartbeat.

She didn't know what she wanted out of life, but there was a part of him that wished it was him she wanted.

The two of them working together in the wilderness would be a perfect team. She could add so much to his practice.

And he could see this whole life unfolding in front of him. The life he wanted with her, but not necessarily the life she wanted.

Thatcher knew all about having a life you didn't want forced upon you, and he was never going to do that to Lacey.

No matter how much he wanted to.

CHAPTER TWELVE

LACEY HAD REALLY thought for a moment a couple of days ago that Thatcher was going to kiss her again at the captain's dinner. Of course he hadn't, though, because they'd had to deal with Raymond's accident on the dance floor at the nightclub.

It was also probably for the best that it didn't happen. Especially not in front of the other officers.

Thatcher didn't seem like the type to attempt public displays of affection.

Although she wished he would've.

She couldn't stop thinking about that moment. She saw the way he was looking at her, and she was feeling the same.

She wanted him.

She might not know what she wanted as her next job or what she wanted in her life besides being a nurse practitioner and midwife, but she knew that she wanted Thatcher, and she'd never wanted a man like this before.

Not even Will.

And she couldn't understand now why she was with Will for the last two years, because her relationship with him had been nothing like this.

She had settled for consistency because it was safe. She'd been so blinded by security that she'd ignored her gut instinct. She had ignored all the red flags.

She'd been a fool.

A lump formed in her throat. She was so annoyed with herself.

The problem was, she didn't want to hold Thatcher back. He might desire her—she had sensed that in his kiss—but he had concrete plans. Plans that he'd been working on since his own heart was broken and he decided to leave his family and title behind.

He had these amazing dreams, and she didn't want to interfere with them. She didn't even know if he wanted her to. What if he just wanted a fling? She wasn't that kind of person, and the uncertainty of it all just gnawed away at her.

And he also didn't know where in the Yukon he wanted to settle. It was all very flighty, and she wasn't comfortable with that.

If only she could figure herself out and figure out what she wanted to do with her life.

The last few days traveling along the Gulf of Alaska had been amazing and quiet. After her checks on a couple of other patients, she walked the deck, trying to work out what she wanted and staring at the vast glaciers and the islands. The forests giving way to tundra and the north. To glaciers and peaks. Stone and sea.

It was beautiful—colder than when they were down in Skagway and Juneau, but it was also very peaceful.

Although the peace wasn't helping her think at all.

This morning, before she made her rounds, there had been a couple more emails from Will, and she still hadn't opened them. She was mad at herself for not facing it, but how could she move forward if she didn't face Will and his infidelity? She couldn't.

She didn't want to hold Thatcher back or hurt him with her uncertainty.

"I thought I'd find you here."

She turned and saw Thatcher walking toward her. Her heart began to beat a bit faster, and she smiled.

"You caught me," she said nervously. "How is Raymond?"

"He's doing good. I don't think he'll need surgery, but he's still going to get himself checked out when we reach Anchorage in a day or so," he said, leaning against the railing beside her.

"I'm glad to hear it." She didn't know what else to say.

She loved being near him, and she resisted the urge to rest her head against his shoulder and watch the world go by.

"I noticed you're not wearing your ring anymore."

Lacey glanced down at her hand. "No, I took it off the night of the captain's dinner."

"You did?"

She blushed. "I did."

Thatcher didn't say anything, and she was disappointed. He cleared his throat. "The captain will be turning around soon, and we'll be heading back to Anchorage. I can't believe this cruise is almost over. These last couple of weeks have flown by."

"They have." She sighed.

"What's wrong?"

"I have a couple of emails from my ex waiting for me in my inbox. I still haven't opened them. My father called me a few days ago and mentioned that my ex was fretting over the fact I hadn't responded."

"What does he expect? He cheated on you."

"Well, he may have actually cheated on me, but how much did I contribute to that? I wasn't exactly the most affectionate person. Maybe I deserved it. I don't think we were ever suited for each other."

"No one deserves a broken heart," Thatcher said sadly.

"My heart doesn't feel that broken, though."

"Maybe he wants some absolution?" Thatcher offered.

She shrugged. She didn't know, but she didn't want to talk about Will or Beth or anything. She just wanted to savor those last few minutes that they were still gliding west toward Unalaska Island before they turned back along the coast and to Anchorage. Once all the passengers were off, they'd be heading to Vancouver, and she would have to make some hard choices about her life.

"I suppose I need to return his ring. Though I don't want to see him."

"Chuck it overboard," Thatcher teased.

She laughed. "No. I guess I'll have to bite the bullet and face him. I'm not reading his emails or calling him today, though. Today I don't want to think of him."

"How about tonight we have dinner again?

Since we didn't get the nice dinner at the captain's table."

The question caught her off guard, but pleased her.

"You're not going to make me dress up again, are you?" she asked.

"No. Actually, I'm not, but the captain is. He's offered us a table in the Upper Deck Restaurant, and it has a dress code."

"Rats, but I guess I can't say no to a dinner that's been offered by Captain Aldridge. Especially if I want to stay in his good graces."

"You've decided to stay on, then?" Thatcher asked.

"No, but I don't want to burn any bridges. Just in case."

"Probably a good idea."

The ship began to slow as the *Alaskan Princess* made its maneuvers to turn around. She caught a last glimpse of Unalaska and, beyond that, the Bering Sea.

The turn of the ship meant a bit of closure, and it made her sad.

"I wish I could go on," she murmured.

"Well, you can. You don't have to stay with this ship. The cruise line has many options. There are cruises that go around the world on even larger ships."

"It's a possibility, but most likely not."

"Well, I have a report to finish. I'll see you at the Upper Deck Restaurant about seven?"

She nodded. "Yes. I'll be there."

He nodded and left.

Lacey sighed and watched as the ship continued its turn. She wasn't the only one watching; most of the ship's passengers were watching the land disappear and the open waters of the Gulf of Alaska take its place.

The sun was starting to set, but it still wouldn't sink below the horizon until about ten at night. The sunlight made her smile.

It was so surreal to see snow and glaciers and have a coat on in August.

She'd forgotten till this trip just how much she loved the north.

She'd forgotten about all those summer nights in Yellowknife. Even the nights when the sun barely set, the nights when the streetlights didn't even have to come on. And she remembered the dark nights of winter, when she and her parents would cuddle up at home as another blizzard howled off Great Slave Lake.

Lacey had locked away all those memories. And as she let them out of the careful box that she kept them in, a tear slipped down her cheek.

She brushed it away, annoyed that she was allowing herself to cry.

That was something she didn't do. Something she hadn't done in a long time.

She straightened herself up and went back to do the last few rounds of check-ins before dinner tonight.

She had a lot to figure out, and crying was something she didn't have time for.

Reminiscing about or mourning something that she couldn't have was pointless.

It would get her nowhere.

Even though she had to wear her little black dress again, because it was the only one she had, she was slightly disappointed when she walked into the restaurant and saw that Thatcher wasn't wearing his white officer's uniform.

She loved the way he looked in that.

Don't let yourself think of him like that.

Only, she couldn't help herself. Even though he wasn't wearing the officer's uniform that she appreciated so much, he still looked good in a dark, well-tailored suit. She couldn't help but wonder if he wore that suit back in England, when he was still the heir and not missing.

It was a shame that he felt like he needed to hide away.

Aren't you doing the same thing?

Hiding away from Will and what had happened. Hiding away from herself. At least she'd taken off the ring. For one brief moment, when Thatcher had suggested it, she'd contemplated tossing it off the side of the ship.

Only, she couldn't.

It wasn't hers anymore. She should return it.

"You look lovely," he said, standing to greet her.

"You do too."

Thatcher pulled out her chair for her. She sat down, and then he sat down. No one she'd been with before had ever pulled out a chair for her; she kind of liked it. Lacey had always done everything on her own, never asked for anything. She took care of herself.

Which was one of Will's gripes, now that she thought about it, because to him it meant that she never took care of him. He'd suggested she was self-centered. Lacey took offense to that. She wasn't self-centered. She'd just been taught to be self-sufficient and not rely on anything or anyone.

Especially not anyone she might get attached to.

It was a scary prospect, getting attached, but a part of her was dreadfully lonely. She'd even been lonely with Will. She just hadn't realized it. She'd ignored it. Just like all the other signs.

She'd grown attached to Thatcher, and she was going to miss him when this was all over.

"I can't believe it's Anchorage tomorrow and the passengers are leaving. I've gotten used to checking on them."

"I know. It's a bit eerie having nothing to do on the voyage home, but it's relaxing."

"Have you heard anything more about Harvey from the hospital in Juneau?" she asked, thinking about the first patient they had worked on together.

"I did. Harvey is awake and doing well. They were able to clear his blocked artery, and hopefully that will resolve his fainting issues."

"Well, that's great news." She was having a hard time coming up with what to talk to him about. All these emotions were running around inside her, and she was trying to get control of them. She hated losing control. She hated this feeling of being so vulnerable in front of him, but it was also a freeing prospect to be her true self and not worry about having to hold anything back.

"I know that I've said it before, but this has been the weirdest, busiest trip I've ever done, and the only new variable is you."

Lacey laughed. "I'm sorry about that, but in a way, I was glad it was slightly busy. It kept my mind off things."

"Like those emails? Have you responded?"

"Have you responded to yours?" she queried back.

"Touché."

The waiter interrupted, poured them wine that Thatcher had ordered before she'd arrived, and then left. There was nothing to order as the restaurant offered a set menu. She took a sip of her wine, suddenly very nervous.

Her stomach was swirling and twisting. Her hands were shaking, and she wished Thatcher's arms were around her right now.

"I need to deal with it," she finally said, not looking at him. "I have to decide what I want to do when this cruise ends, because I don't know. At least you have it all figured out."

"Partly," he said gently. "I know the general direction I want to go, but I don't know where I'll be settling and when I'll be able to get my practice up and running or even if the territorial government will let me. I hope they will. I have all my visas, but there's still a process."

Lacey was surprised. "So you're rushing to the Yukon blind and without a backup?"

"I suppose I am," he said.

"That's kind of crazy," she admitted.

"It is, but it's what I've always wanted. I want to make it work. I love Canada, and I love the

Yukon territory. It's where I want to be, and I'm willing to do whatever it takes to make it work."

"And what if you have to leave?" she asked.

"It'll break my heart, but I'll deal with it as it comes."

And there it was. She wasn't sure that she could latch onto something or someone with the threat that it might all be lost to her. She'd experienced that pain before, and she wasn't willing to go through it again.

It was better to play it safe.

"I'm not sure I could ever take a risk like that," she admitted.

"Yes, but what is that saying I heard once? There is no growth in a comfort zone."

"Perhaps not, but at least there's safety."

The waiter returned with their food, but Lacey couldn't really focus on it. Her emotions were everywhere, and she wasn't really hungry. It was like the world was spinning, and she just wanted to get off the ride. The food was like a lump of tasteless nothing in her mouth, and it was hard to swallow.

She couldn't breathe. All she could think of was everything she had lost.

And how she'd soon lose Thatcher.

It was too much.

"Lacey?" Thatcher asked. "Are you all right?"

"No. I don't think that I am," she said quietly. "I think I'm having a bit of a panic attack."

Thatcher stood up. "Come on. You need some air."

She stood up, and Thatcher put his arm around her; it was reassuring. They headed out of the restaurant, onto the deck. It was getting dark, but it was still warm since the deck was covered, and they could see outside.

Still, she shivered, and Thatcher pulled her closer.

"Sorry," she said, trying to catch her breath. "I don't know what happened."

"It's okay," he said gently. "You've been through a lot."

"We both have," she said. "I don't know what came over me. It's weird that we're coming to the end of this."

"It's okay, and it is odd. Trust me."

Lacey smiled. "I do, which is a huge thing for me. I don't trust easy, especially those I don't know well. Will isn't the first to have cheated on me. I've been hurt too much. Lost too much."

Thatcher smiled. "Same. Did you actually trust your ex-fiancé, though? Because something tells me that you didn't. Not really."

"You're right. I didn't. I don't even know why I was with him, to be honest." She sighed. "It just seemed like the right thing to do, and when

I saw him with the woman I thought was my best friend, I left. But I didn't cry. I…don't know why."

"Because you weren't even angry?"

"I was, but… I didn't say anything. What kind of person doesn't say anything in that situation?" She could feel tears welling in her eyes. "Am I that unfeeling? Am I that uncaring?"

"I don't know," Thatcher said softly. "I questioned myself when my relationship with Kathleen ended. I was crushed. I felt betrayed. She thought I was going to be the duke, and maybe it was shallow, but I wasn't the person she thought I was supposed to be, so maybe in a way I betrayed her too. I don't know."

It touched her heart that he was opening up to her like this.

Why was it that she could be herself with him? Why did she let all these emotions out around him?

What kind of hold did he have on her?

She glanced up at the sky above her and could see stars through the glass. So many stars, just like the sky she'd seen when she was a little girl.

"Wow," she whispered. She'd been so busy on this cruise that at night she just went to bed and slept. She hadn't looked up at the sky since that night after their first kiss. It calmed her. Just like it had done that night.

In Vancouver, Lacey didn't see the sky. On the odd sunny day, she'd look up at the blue, but it had been a long time since she'd paid attention to the night sky.

And suddenly all she could think about was her friend Carol. She remembered them lying in her backyard in the middle of the night in late August, staring at the sky.

All the stars.

"It's kind of amazing. Another reason I love the north. There is no artificial light drowning out the night sky. I'll never get tired of this."

Lacey nodded. "Yes, I'd forgotten. It's been so long. When I was a little girl, I would spend many nights just staring up at the sky. I turned away from the sky when I moved to Vancouver."

And as if the sky was acknowledging her back, a small ribbon of light wound its way across the stars, faint at first, like ink in water. It was bright green, and she smiled as it moved, rippling and flowing above her.

She could hear other people who were out and about, watching like she was. She could hear their gasps, but she kept silent, watching in awe as that thin little ribbon turned thicker and pushed its way across the sky, erupting into beautiful waves of green stretching up above her.

It had been a long time since she'd seen the aurora borealis.

Too long.

All that anxiety she'd been feeling melted away. All she felt was joy and connection. She'd been living in a fog for too long. It was as though Carol was reaching out to speak to her again.

"I'm so glad we saw them," Thatcher whispered.

"Me too. It's perfect." Lacey looked up at him, his head turned toward the sky as he watched, but then he looked down at her, his gray eyes twinkling.

Just like that night they had shared their first kiss. Lacey wanted to kiss him again. Her body was thrumming with need. She'd wanted him from the moment she first saw him, and she knew that if they kissed this time, she wasn't going to stop. She wouldn't be able to stop. Lacey wanted Thatcher, and even though their journeys in life weren't on the same paths, she was going to experience this time together with him to its fullest.

Thatcher was right. Nothing grew out of a comfort zone, and she was going to take this one small leap, just this one time, and see where it led.

"You are more beautiful than the northern lights," Thatcher said, touching her cheek gently. "I know I shouldn't be saying it, but I can't help myself."

"Why shouldn't you be saying it?" she asked.

"Because neither of us can promise each other

something, and you made it clear the first night we kissed that nothing can come of it. I don't want to make you uncomfortable."

"You're not." And then she leaned forward and kissed him gently. "You're not making me uncomfortable, and I know you can't promise me anything, but that's okay. I just want tonight."

"Tonight?" he asked, confused.

"Yes. Just tonight. I just want tonight." And then she kissed him again, letting him know exactly what she wanted out of tonight.

This time with Thatcher was fleeting.

For one night, under the northern lights, she wanted to live.

To feel again, with him.

Thatcher wanted her more than anything. It had been something he'd been fighting for weeks.

He knew she had a lot to deal with, and there was a part of him that wasn't sure he could really open his heart to someone again, but he was lonely, and he wanted her. It burned his soul, his need to have her, but he didn't want to rush her or push her. That was not his style, so he'd just desired her from afar. Pined for her, knowing nothing would probably happen.

And then she kissed him. A kiss that burned him right down to his very soul. His body yearned for her, to hold her and kiss her.

To claim her as his own.

Only, he couldn't have her. She wasn't his to claim. She'd made that clear, and he had plans too, but for tonight, if she wanted, he would happily be with her and let his desire rule his mind and his heart.

"Lacey," he murmured against her neck.

"Please, Thatcher," she whispered, before kissing him again. "I know nothing can come from this, but I also know I want this."

Lacey took his hand and pulled him away from their dark little corner of the deck, toward the stairway leading down to the staff quarters. If only they had had dinner in his cabin so he could've scooped her up in his arms and carried her to bed.

Getting from above to below deck took forever in his mind, but he knew it would be worth it. His pulse was racing with anticipation, his body reacting to the promise that soon she would be his. Even if only for one night.

His quarters were the closest, so that's where they went. His heart was in his throat, his blood burning as he opened the door.

Once they were on the other side and the door was shut, those kisses that had been controlled up on the deck were let loose.

He pressed her against the wall, his hands in her hair. Devouring her.

He broke the kiss off. "Are you sure, Lacey?"

Even though he was burning for her—desired her, needed her—if she changed her mind, he'd let her go.

He was all in, though.

More than all in. He was close to losing his heart if he wasn't careful.

"I'm sure," she whispered, her voice trembling. She took his hand and pressed it against her chest. He could feel her pulse racing under his fingertips.

Her skin was like satin. Soft. Smooth.

And she burned hot. For him.

He liked that dress she wore, but now he needed her out of it. Thatcher wanted nothing between them. He wanted to run his hands over her, his lips. He wanted to be a part of her.

Lacey nuzzled his neck, the press of her lips against him making a zing of awareness course through his body.

Her fingers worked the buttons of his shirt while he unzipped her dress.

He just wanted her naked and pressed against him.

That's all he wanted.

Just her.

There was no fighting it anymore.

He was lost to her.

* * *

Lacey couldn't ever recall being so consumed with passion before.

She'd never had this burning need for someone, but with Thatcher it was a craving. She wanted him. Needed him.

Lacey just wanted to forget about it all.

She couldn't get her clothes off fast enough.

"You're so beautiful," Thatcher said again when it was just her, naked in front of him.

She found she wasn't embarrassed. She pulled him flush against her body.

"Touch me," she murmured, guiding his hand up to her breasts. It made her blood sing, her body come alive for the first time in a long time. And she wanted more as Thatcher pressed her against his bed, his lips branding hot flames against her skin. She arched her back, trying to get closer to him, her body tingling and every nerve seeming to wake back up after a long sleep.

A shiver of anticipation coursed through her.

It was so good.

"I want you, Lacey," he murmured.

"Feel how much I need you." She opened her legs, thrusting her hips up at him.

He growled possessively, his hands hot and heavy on her skin.

Thatcher's hand slipped between her legs, stroking her. She gasped, crying out.

Her body was thrumming with need for him.

"Do you have protection?" she asked.

"I do." He reached over and pulled a condom out of his nightstand drawer.

"Let me help you with that." She tore open the packet and slowly rolled the condom down over his shaft. Thatcher moaned as she stroked him. He was at her mercy.

"Oh, God, Lacey."

"What?" she teased breathlessly. "What're you going to do?"

He grinned, grabbing her hands and pinning her wrists down as he thrust into her, making her cry out.

Thatcher moved slowly, so slowly, and she urged him to go faster. She wanted all of him, and she wanted it now. He thrust hard against her, over and over as a coil of heat unfurled in her belly. Pleasure overtaking her.

She wrapped her legs around him, not wanting him to move or leave her as she came, and it wasn't long before he cried out, coming right after her.

Her body was like a puddle of Jell-O, and it was good to just be in his arms.

It couldn't be forever, but it could be for tonight.

CHAPTER THIRTEEN

WHEN THATCHER WOKE up in the morning, he realized the ship had stopped, and as he rubbed his eyes, he could see the blurry cityscape of Anchorage in the distance through the open drapes.

Lacey was still sleeping soundly, her bottom warm against him, and all he wanted to do was stay snuggled in bed with her. He couldn't remember the last time he'd slept so soundly. In fact, he wasn't sure that he had ever slept like this before.

She made him happy, and he wished they had more time together.

Thatcher gently kissed her cheek. "We're in Anchorage."

Lacey opened her eyes slowly. "We are?"

"Yes. I'm afraid we're going to have to get up and do our job as the passengers disembark in a couple of hours."

Lacey stretched. "I suppose so."

As much as he didn't want to get up, he knew

they had to. They weren't the ones on vacation, after all. Lacey climbed out of bed and began gathering up her clothes to get dressed, which was a real shame in Thatcher's opinion.

Lacey finished pulling on her clothes. "I'll see you later?"

"Yes. Make sure you wear your white uniform."

"Oh. Joy." She leaned over and kissed him. "Thank you for last night."

"Thank *you*."

Thatcher pulled her down and kissed her again. She laughed and pushed him away, slipping out of his room.

He lay back and stared up at the ceiling, and all he could do was smile. But then it struck him that soon this would be over, and he'd be on his way to the Yukon.

Alone.

He sighed and got up to get ready, washing up and then dressing in his white uniform to prepare for the departing passengers. Thatcher didn't want to think about Lacey leaving.

She's not leaving. You are.

And he had to keep reminding himself of that. This was only supposed to be a temporary thing. That was it.

He wasn't going to hold Lacey back. The last time he tried to have a woman follow along with his plans, it had gone spectacularly badly and left him brokenhearted.

Lacey isn't Kathleen, though.

Lacey was different.

Still, she had just come out of a serious relationship. She didn't know what she wanted out of life, and she deserved the chance to figure it all out, without him trying to sway her. When they had kissed again and she told him that she wanted him, she told him that it would only be for one night.

And he had to accept that, even if he didn't want to.

He locked up his quarters and made his way along the hall to head to the upper decks. As he passed other members of the crew, they stared at him, which made him uneasy. He smiled, but something was bothering him about the way they were looking at him.

It sent a chill down his spine.

He headed above deck and saw a group of officers mingling by the door where passengers were slowly disembarking. As he approached, he saw Lacey in the crowd, looking distressed. As he waved to passengers leaving, he realized the passengers were looking at him with what he could only describe as awe.

A shiver of dread coursed through his blood, and he stared at the pile of complimentary newspapers that was sitting at the check-in desk of the ship.

On the front cover of the paper was a photo of him…and Lacey.

A photograph of them on the train in Skagway, or rather, a photograph of them on the train at the White Pass, and the headline read, The Missing Heir Has Been Found.

"Thatcher," Lacey said, rushing over.

He picked up a paper in disbelief, just staring at it.

For five years he'd managed to keep his identity secret, but the one time he went back up the White Pass and decided to step outside the train car to enjoy the ride with a woman, someone from the other car had recognized him and snapped a picture.

He was upset.

No, he was livid.

"Your Grace, I had no idea that we had such a celebrity serving on the *Alaskan Princess*. A bit beneath you, isn't it?" Matt said, taking the chance to scoff while the captain wasn't around.

Thatcher saw red, but he wasn't going to lower himself to the first officer's level, so he turned on his heel, storming off.

Lacey followed him.

"Thatcher!"

He couldn't turn around. He had to figure out

what to do, and he wasn't sure what that might be. He headed straight for the infirmary to collect his thoughts, and as he stared at the newspaper he saw there was more.

There was information about Lacey—about her jilting her fiancé and leaving him at the altar.

And there was information about Thatcher's father being on his deathbed.

It made his blood run cold. He tossed the paper to the side as Lacey entered the infirmary and shut the door behind her.

He didn't really want to see her, but he knew she was probably reeling from the insinuations made against her, the claims she had jilted her ex for a duke. What the world didn't know was that Lacey didn't know he was a duke when she ran away from her ex. Not that it would matter much if they told anyone.

The world would believe what they wanted to believe.

He was sorry that he ever got involved with Lacey and caused her name to be dragged through the proverbial mud.

"I'm so sorry," Lacey said, staring at the paper.

"Why? It's not your fault. You didn't tell anyone. And they slandered your name too."

"I know," she said quietly. "They can say what they want. My family knows the truth. I didn't leave Will for a duke. And also, you're not a duke."

He gave her a half smile. She was trying to make things lighter, but he didn't feel like making light of the situation.

"My father is ill," he stated.

"Did you know that or is this news?"

"I knew. Michael called me right before we left and told me Father was sick and wanted me to come home. I ignored him."

"And you didn't respond to the email from your father, did you?"

He shook his head. "No."

"What're you going to do?"

"Nothing."

"Nothing?" she asked. "What if your father is actually dying?"

"I don't want to be duke."

"Yeah, but that doesn't change the fact that your father could be dying, and this is your only chance to make things right with him."

"You don't know what you're talking about. You won't even face your ex," he snapped back.

Lacey frowned and crossed her arms. "He's not dying. And I'm headed back to Vancouver next week anyway."

"Lacey, come on. You don't know what you want. Who's to say you won't run away again? You shut people out."

"I'm not the only one running."

"What do you mean?"

"You've been hiding these last five years."

He narrowed his eyes and glared at her. "You have no concept of the life I would have to lead, the life I would have to give up to take my birthright. I don't want that."

"Sometimes we have to do things that we don't want to do."

"Like marrying a man you don't love? Because wasn't that what you were going to do?"

Lacey glared at him. "Why are you turning on me? What have I done to you?"

He ran a hand through his hair. "Nothing. Nothing."

"You're lashing out irrationally."

"It's because I love you."

Her eyes opened wide in shock, and she took a step back. "What?"

"I said that I love you. I want you to stay with me."

She shook her head, looking terrified. "No. No you don't. You can't. We've only known each other for a few weeks. There is no way that you can… You can't love me."

"I do," he said fiercely. "And if I have to face this inevitable fate as a duke, I want you to go with me."

"You're insane."

"Lacey, I want you with me."

She shook her head and backed up. "I can't do that, Thatcher. I can't do that. I don't want that life."

"How do you know?"

Her brow furrowed. "You don't even want that life. Why would I want that kind of life?"

"Because you love me too."

He said it with hope, but he knew she was scared, and he was frantic. Everything was changing so fast.

"Thatcher... I can't. I just..." She turned to leave, but he stood in front of her, blocking her exit.

"You're going to run again?"

She glared at him. "I don't know you."

"You do know me. You're just afraid. Afraid to take a chance."

"I'm not the only one afraid," she snapped. "You're afraid of being alone. You come to Canada to hide away and lick your wounds, saying you want some kind of life in the north, but really you'll go back and become the Duke of Weymouth because you can't stand up to your father and tell him that you don't want your birthright."

"You don't understand what you're talking about."

"I understand. You lashed out at me because you need someone to blame."

Her words stung like a slap. "And what about you? You're so afraid of anything. You say that you're envious of my plans, that I know where I'm going. Well, you have the whole world open to you. You can do whatever you want, be whoever you want, but you don't do that. You just follow your parents around blindly."

"Get out of my way." Her voice quivered, and he hated hurting her, but he was angry. Kathleen had only wanted him when he was going to be a duke, and Lacey didn't want him for the same reason.

The thing was, Thatcher wasn't even sure that she would want him if he didn't take his title. Even if he went to the Yukon and pursued his plan, he wasn't sure that she would follow him. Once again, he'd put his heart on the line, and the woman he'd fallen for had crushed it.

He'd been a fool thinking that Lacey was different; he should've known better when he first laid eyes on her in that wedding dress, fresh from jilting her ex-fiancé.

She couldn't even deal with her hurt from that.

She had locked away all her emotions. Like he should've done.

Thatcher stepped to the side. Lacey opened

the door and left the infirmary, slamming the door behind her.

All he could do was stand there.

He was angry at himself for falling in love again and for putting his heart on the line. Thatcher understood what he had to do, now that the world knew exactly where he was. He picked up the phone and made a call.

It would be six in the evening, and he hoped that Michael would be there.

"Weymouth Manor," the butler's voice said over the crackling line.

"Heath, it's Edward. I would like to speak to Michael."

"Very good, my lord. Please hold the line."

Thatcher waited, his pulse thundering in his ears.

"Edward?" Michael asked in amazement.

"Yes."

"You actually called."

"Well, since the secret is out, there is no need to hide."

"You're coming home?" Michael asked.

"I am. Can you arrange a flight for me out of Anchorage?"

"Anchorage? You're not in Vancouver?"

"No. I'm going to disembark here in Anchorage after I speak to the captain, but I'm sure it will be fine. The world knows where I am, and

I'm sure there will be press waiting in Vancouver. If I fly from Anchorage, I may be able to avoid all that."

"I'll arrange a car to come to the port in about an hour," Michael said.

"Tell me one thing," Thatcher said, his voice breaking slightly. "Is Father really dying?"

Michael sighed. "It doesn't look good. He's emailed you several times. He thought you might never come home and wants to make amends."

"Well, tell him I'm on the next flight out of Anchorage."

"Tickets will be waiting at the airport," Michael said. "I'll have a car meet you at Heathrow when you arrive."

"Thank you."

"I'll see you soon."

Thatcher ended the call. When he woke up this morning, he'd thought that he would have another week with Lacey, and a part of him had hoped he could convince her to spend her life with him.

For one brief moment, he'd felt like there was hope and that he could put his heart in the hands of another.

How wrong he'd been.

Lacey paced in her room, trying to process everything that had happened in the infirmary.

He says he loves me.

Only, she couldn't quite believe that, and she felt a dread inside her, because she knew she loved him too. She was terrified by that prospect.

How could he love her?

It felt like her heart was going to burst.

Why did she let this go so far?

Why did she open up her heart when she didn't even know what she wanted? She felt like crying, and there was a knot deep in the pit of her stomach she couldn't shake.

She hated herself. She hated that she was so afraid.

Even too afraid to open the numerous messages from Will.

It would be so simple. Why couldn't she face it?

Maybe Thatcher was right. She was just running away from all of her problems.

He says he loves me.

But being with him might mean packing up and moving to England to become a duchess. She might not know what she wanted, but she knew she didn't want that. She took this job to have an adventure and to clear her head so that she could figure out what she wanted in life. Instead, she ran smack-dab into a Prince Charming of sorts. Tears welled up in her eyes as she thought about him. She had gone to the infirmary to console him because his secret was out and it was partly her fault—it was because of her he was on the train over the White Pass and got spotted—but it had all gone horribly wrong.

She shook her head.

She had been so afraid for so long to put real trust in someone or something else.

What if Thatcher took her to England, and she wasn't good enough? What if they got married, but she hated it there and their marriage ended? What if she couldn't have children for the lineage?

There were so many things she was uncertain about. And then she remembered what Thatcher had said about things not growing in a comfort zone.

She saw now how true those words were.

The thing was, she'd never asked these questions when she was with Will, because it really never mattered. Not the way it did with Thatcher.

A tear slid down her cheek as it hit her.

She was really in love with Thatcher. She had liked Will well enough; what they had was comfortable, and she was willing to marry him because he was stable. But with Thatcher, there was this level of the unknown, and she was terrified about what the future might hold. It was a risk. One she had never been willing to take a chance on because she was afraid of all the ups and downs of love.

She was so afraid of having her heart broken in the process of trying to find someone she would be truly happy with, that she had actually broken her own heart. Lacey had pushed away love with Thatcher because she didn't know what the future held, and she was so scared of losing him.

Lacey broke down crying.

Something she hadn't done in so long.

Everything she had been holding on to came out in a flood of tears.

Her life flashed before her eyes, and she mourned her friends up north, her home, each move her family had made. She had swallowed all of that pain away until she was so full she was numb.

Now the only way to deal with it was to let it out.

Tears transitioned into great heaving sobs, and when her storm of emotion finally subsided, she wiped her tears away and picked up her phone to read the email messages from Will.

He asked for her forgiveness and said everything that she had come to realize for herself. That they hadn't really been in love, that marriage just seemed like the right thing to do, and when Lacey was so distant with him, because they had no real connection, he took solace in Beth's company. They had connected and eventually fallen in love.

He apologized for her finding them like that, said it wasn't supposed to happen and he was on his way to end the marriage when she'd walked in. He had planned to leave her at the altar, but she got there first.

Lacey swallowed the lump in her throat and replied that she forgave him and agreed with him. She let Will know that it was okay. And then emailed Beth to say the same.

And it was.

That's why she'd been numb to what happened, because it didn't hurt. She didn't care.

She did care about someone, though, and she'd just turned down his offer of a happiness she'd never thought she'd find.

Not that she wanted to live in England, but Lacey realized it wasn't a place that was home; home was the person that you loved. That was why she'd followed her parents for so long— she'd found her home in their love.

But now she needed to move on. She needed to put down her own roots—make her own home—and she wanted to do that with Thatcher.

She quickly washed her face and headed out

into the hall just as the ship started to move, pulling away from Anchorage.

She made her way back to the infirmary, but when she got there, all of Thatcher's things were gone. His computer, his mug. Everything.

Her stomach knotted, and she left the infirmary, heading to his quarters. But when she got there, one of the housekeeping staff was inside, and she could see his room had been stripped.

"Where is Dr. Bell?"

The cleaner looked up. "He disembarked in Anchorage."

"What?" Lacey asked, panicked.

"He asked the captain if he could leave. Apparently his father is dying, and he's going to be the new Duke of Weymouth!" the woman said excitedly. "He was flying straight out."

Lacey nodded numbly and left his room, her heart breaking.

She'd ruined it.

Ruined her best chance at happiness.

Thatcher had left her.

And now she had no way to get a hold of him to tell him that she loved him too. She was stuck on this ship for a week, but she knew what she needed to do to make things right once she got to Vancouver.

She might not be able to stop him at the gate, but she was going to fly to England and tell him she loved him. Even if he rejected her, she would take a chance for once in her life, because her future was nothing without him.

CHAPTER FOURTEEN

Two weeks later, England

THATCHER SAT IN the study at Weymouth Manor, watching the drizzle outside through the window. If he squinted his eyes enough, he could pretend that he was on the ship going up the inside passage, except that it was manicured lawns and farmland beyond the stone fences of his father's manor.

He'd rather be back on the ship or in the Yukon.

That was a lie.

He'd rather be back in Lacey's arms than anywhere else. She might have rejected him and run scared, but he knew deep down that Lacey loved him. She was just afraid.

And he could be patient.

Except, he wasn't sure where she was. He'd tried calling the only Greenwoods listed in Vancouver, but there had been no response, and he didn't leave a message.

There was a knock at the door.

"Come," Thatcher said, swiveling in his chair.

Michael came into the study. "Your letter was received, renouncing your title."

Thatcher took a deep breath. "And Father is okay with this?"

Michael nodded. "He just wants you in his life. I know he was absent when we were kids, but he's changed. He's trying to make amends. You've just been too stubborn to listen the last couple of years."

Thatcher smiled. "I know."

He'd been stubborn about a lot of things. When he'd arrived back at Weymouth Manor a couple of weeks ago, brokenhearted and tired from his trip, he'd been shocked at how warmly he'd been received and the apologies his father had been making.

Thatcher had always thought he was so different from his father, but he wasn't.

They were cut from the same cloth.

In stubbornness, anyhow.

And it was that stubborn streak that may have cost him the love of his life. He'd been a fool, but there was nothing he could do about it just yet. He was stuck here because he had to wait until the title was officially renounced before he could go to the Yukon. The thing was, he wasn't sure he wanted to go to the Yukon alone.

Ultimately, he wanted Lacey and would do anything to have her in his life.

"Are you sure this is what you want?" Michael asked, his hands in his pockets.

"Yes," Thatcher said. "I want to be a physician. I've never wanted to manage land or attend functions or have a seat in the House of Lords. All that bores me to tears, but you…you love that. And what's more, you are good at it. You were born to be the duke. Not me."

Michael nodded. "Well, I'm happy to take it on. Weymouth Manor has always meant so much to me. As have you. These last five years without you in my life—and me wondering where in the bloody hell you've been—have been awful."

"I'm sorry, Michael."

Michael cocked his eyebrow and sternly looked down his nose at Thatcher, which seemed to be a trait for all successful dukes in this family.

"Well, you better come back and visit from time to time. Don't expect me to go to the Yukon. I have no idea why you love it there so much."

"Neither do I." Thatcher sighed. "But I do."

There was another knock at the door, and Heath entered the room. "I'm sorry, my lords. There is a young lady from Canada here to see you," he said, addressing Thatcher.

His heart skipped a beat, and he stood up. "What?"

Heath looked at him. "A young lady from Canada, or more importantly, someone by the name of Lacey, sir."

Michael looked back at him. "Is this the girl you were moping about?"

Thatcher ignored him. "Show her to the sitting room, Heath, and I'll be there in a moment."

"Very good, my lord." Heath left.

"Is this the woman you fell in love with?" Michael asked.

"Yes. Although I'm worried she's changed her mind and wants to be a duchess. Like Kathleen."

Michael gave him a look. "I seriously doubt that, if she's anything like the way you've described her."

"Well, she doesn't know that I rescinded the title."

"I don't think she's here for a title. If she's the woman you said she is, then she's here for you. You are worthy of love, Thatcher. With or without a title. You're an honorable and decent man. Kathleen was a gold digger. Go find out why your Canadian is here and take your chance."

Thatcher nodded and left the study.

His stomach was in knots as he made his way to the sitting room.

Heath had left the door open, and he saw she

was standing in the middle of the room, her mouth open as she looked at his father's paintings adorning the walls, some from the masters.

"Lacey," he said, taking a step into the room.

She spun around. Her cheeks bloomed with pink. "Thatcher."

"What're you doing here?"

Lacey had been so nervous. When she got off the cruise ship in Vancouver, she'd declined continuing with the job and made her way over to her parents' to collect herself and pack. She was going to England, but first she had to do some reconnaissance and figure out where in England he was.

She found out where Weymouth Manor was and then packed for her trip, getting the earliest flight she could.

After a couple of connections and a delayed flight, she landed in England, rented a car, had a quick lesson about driving on the left and then made her way to Weymouth Manor to tell Thatcher that she wanted him.

If that meant she had to live in England, then fine.

All she wanted and needed was Thatcher.

She was so in love with him, and though she'd been scared to let herself love him—because she wasn't sure that she could handle the pain if she ever lost him—she also knew she couldn't spend the rest of her life living in fear and not taking chances.

So here she was, standing in a sitting room that was a bit overwhelming, her heart pounding in her throat. She suddenly felt like that movie she'd watched a long time ago where the heroine had said something about a girl being in front of a boy... She couldn't remember the words exactly, but she suddenly understood how that girl felt.

"I've come to apologize," she said, finally finding her voice.

"For what?" he asked.

"For saying that you were wrong, and for saying that I don't love you, because you were absolutely right. I was afraid. I was running away and...and I love you." She tried to swallow past the lump in her throat, her hands shaking as she waited for his response.

He turned and shut the door to the sitting room behind him. "You love me?"

"I do. And if we have to live here so you can take your title, then okay."

He paused. "Are you only back here because of my title? Do you only want me because of that?"

"No. I honestly would hate being a duchess, and I would make the worst duchess ever. You don't know how many people in this country already hate me—I'm sure I probably pissed off a dozen of your tenants driving on the right accidentally a few times and almost hitting a sheep or two on the way here. I would not be good at this life, but I know one thing."

"What's that?" he asked, the hint of a smile appearing on his face.

"My life wouldn't be whole without you. I love you, Thatcher. My life isn't complete without you in it."

He smiled and closed the gap between them, taking her in his arms and kissing her. The kiss seared her blood and made her heart sing.

"I love you, Lacey Greenwood, even if you would make a lousy duchess. But you don't have to worry about that."

"I don't?" she asked.

"I gave up my title. My brother, Michael, who is much more suited to the task, is going to take over the title when my father dies...which won't be for a while yet. He's doing much better."

"You're not going to be the duke?"

"No," he said seriously, his arms around her. "Do you still want me? Do you think that you could live a life with just a simple physician?"

She sighed and smiled. "Yes. I think I can. You know I love the north."

"It doesn't have to be the Yukon. I can go anywhere."

Lacey shook her head. "No, the Yukon. That's where you wanted to go, and I would love to live back in the north. As long as you'll have me as your nurse practitioner and midwife still, then I'll follow you anywhere. I can't live without you. You are my home, Thatcher. It's not a place that makes a home or roots. It's the person you share your life with."

He smiled and picked her up, spinning her around. "I love you, Lacey. Marry me. Now. Before you decide to run away on me."

She laughed. "Fine, but isn't it kind of hard to get married quickly here? I mean, don't we need a special license or something…"

"My father can handle it. He has some connections with the archbishop. We'll get married here. Then, as soon as my visa comes in, we'll go to Vancouver, get your things and drive up to the Yukon. Does that sound like a future you can live with?"

Lacey smiled. "Yes, my lord. I think I can handle a future like that."

Thatcher kissed her again, and it felt like her heart was going to burst.

"Let's go tell my father and brother. Oh, and I'll let him know there are a few tenants he'll have to buy off."

Lacey laughed and took his hand. They left the sitting room to make their way up the stairs so that she could meet her future father-in-law, the Duke of Weymouth.

She'd always been afraid of her future, but with Thatcher by her side, she was no longer scared about what that future held.

For the first time ever, she was looking forward to finding out.

EPILOGUE

One year later, Stewart River, Yukon Territory

LACEY STEPPED OUTSIDE onto the deck of the log cabin she'd helped Thatcher build in a small town that was nestled between Dawson City and Whitehorse. The summer breeze felt good; it had been unusually hot for late August.

The clinic had been busy, and she would have to make her way into the small town soon to do a couple of home checks on some pregnant patients.

Thatcher was chopping wood to get ready for the winter, which was coming fast, and Lacey smiled, watching him.

She had just finished cleaning their guest room for her parents' arrival in a week.

She had something exciting to tell them, but first she had to let Thatcher know. It was something they had talked about, but hadn't really planned for yet.

"Do you have a minute?" Lacey asked, walking down the steps.

"Yes." He sank his ax into the log. "You leaving soon for town?"

"Soon, but not yet." She smiled and found she was just as nervous as that day when she'd shown up at Weymouth Manor and bared her heart to him. "I need to show you something."

"Sure."

She handed him a sheet of paper that had her blood results on it. She'd run the test herself, sending it off to the lab as it was hard to come by a simple pregnancy test up here.

"You took a blood test?" he asked, confused.

"Yes, take a look and tell me what you think."

He cocked an eyebrow and glanced at the sheet. "Cholesterol looks good."

"Yes, but look closer."

He was scanning the paper, and she knew the moment he saw it, because his eyes opened wide and he stared at it closer. "HcG?"

"Yes." She laughed nervously. "About eight weeks."

"Are you serious?" he asked in disbelief.

"Yes. Are you happy?"

"More than happy." He scooped her up in his arms and kissed her.

"Well, now you can see why I'm so anxious for my parents to come. I want to tell them in person that they'll be grandparents. We'll have to video chat your father soon too and let him know."

Thatcher kissed her again. "We will, but first I plan to take you in that cabin and show you just how happy you've made me."

"What about the firewood?"

"Who cares?" he said huskily.

"I have patients."

"Not until later. For the next couple of hours, you're mine, Nurse Bell."

He kissed her, and she laughed as he carried her over the threshold into their happy-ever-after.

* * * * *

If you enjoyed this story, check out these other great reads from Amy Ruttan

Falling for the Billionaire Doc
Twin Surprise for the Baby Doctor
A Reunion, a Wedding, a Family
Reunited with Her Hot-Shot Surgeon

All available now!